M. C. Beaton is the author of both the Agatha Raisin and Hamish Macbeth series, as well as numerous Regency romances. Her Agatha Raisin books have been turned into a TV series on Sky 1. She lives in Paris and in a Cotswolds village that is very much like Agatha's beloved Carsely.

The Hamish Macbeth series

DEATH
OF A BORE

A HAMISH MACBETH MURDER MYSTERY

M. C. BEATON

CONSTABLE

CONSTABLE

First published in the United States in 2006 by Grand Central Publishing,
a division of Hachette Book Group USA, Inc.

First published in Great Britain in 2010 by Robinson,
an imprint of Constable & Robinson Ltd.

This edition published in Great Britain in 2018 by Constable

1 3 5 7 9 10 8 6 4 2

A CIP catalogue record for this book
is available from the British Library.

ISBN: 978-1-47212-456-2

Typeset in Palatino by Photoprint
Printed and bound in Great Britain by
CPI Group (UK) Ltd, Croydon CR0 4YY

Papers used by Constable are from well-managed forests and other
responsible sources.

Constable
An imprint of
Little, Brown Book Group
Carmelite House
50 Victoria Embankment
London EC4Y 0DZ

An Hachette UK Company
www.hachette.co.uk

www.littlebrown.co.uk

For Alistair and Amanda Locke of Inverness
With affection

Chapter One

No man, but a blockhead, ever wrote,
except for money.
                              – Samuel Johnson

There used to be quite a lot going on in a highland village during the long, dark winter
months. There was a ceilidh every week where
the locals danced or performed, singing the
old songs or reciting poetry. Often there was a
sewing circle with its attendant gossip; the
Mothers' Union meetings; the Girl Guides and
Boy Scouts classes; and the weekly film show
in the village hall. But with the advent of television and videos, people often preferred to
stay cosily indoors, being amused by often
violent films with heroines with high cheek-
bones, collagen-enhanced lips, and heels so
high it made ankles comfortably ending in
slippered feet just ache to look at them.

Therefore when Hamish Macbeth, police
constable of Lochdubh, heard that a newcomer, John Heppel, was planning to hold a

series of writers' classes in the village hall, he set out to dissuade him. As he said to his fisherman friend, Archie Maclean, 'I don't want to see the poor wee man humiliated when nobody turns up.'

Hamish had seen a poster in Patel's general store: DO YOU WANT TO BE A FAMOUS WRITER? FAMOUS WRITER JOHN HEPPEL WILL HELP YOU BECOME ONE.

The first meeting was scheduled for the following week on a Wednesday evening at seven-thirty. Hamish knew that on that evening *Petticoat Cops* was showing at just that time, a cop series set in LA with three leggy blondes with large lips, high busts, and an amazing skill with firearms and kung fu. He did not know anyone in Lochdubh who would risk missing the latest episode, except perhaps himself.

So on one wet black evening with a gusty gale blowing in from the Atlantic and ragged clouds ripping across the sky, Hamish got into the police Land Rover and set out for John's cottage, which was out on the moors above the village of Cnothan. Hamish was feeling lonely. His affair with the local reporter, Elspeth Grant, had come to an abrupt halt. She had been offered a job on a Glasgow newspaper and had asked him bluntly if he meant to marry her.

And Hamish had dithered, then he had said he'd think about it, and by the time he had got around to really considering the idea, Elspeth had accepted the job and left. He wondered gloomily whether he was cut out to live with anyone, for his first feeling on hearing the news that she had gone was one of relief.

He wondered at first why John had not decided to hold his classes in Cnothan but then reflected that Cnothan was a sour town and specialized in ostracizing newcomers.

Sergeant MacGregor, who had policed Cnothan for years, had retired, and the village and surrounding area had been added on to Hamish's already extensive beat. Village police stations were being closed down all over the place, and Hamish had not felt strong enough to protest at the extra work in case he lost his beloved home in the police station in Lochdubh.

Hamish had never met John Heppel. Normally he would have made a courtesy call, but an irritating series of burglaries over in Braikie had to be solved, and somehow the man's arrival in the Highlands had gone out of his mind. Much as he loved Sutherland and could not consider living anywhere else, Hamish knew that newcomers often relocated to the far north of Scotland through misguided romanticism. Writers or painters imagined that the solitude and wild scenery would inspire them, but usually it was the very long dark winters that finally defeated them.

He drove through Cnothan, bleak and rain-swept under the orange glare of sodium lights, and up on to the moors. The heathery track leading to John's cottage had a poker-work sign pointing the way. It said, 'Writer's Folly'.

Hamish drove along the track and parked outside the low whitewashed cottage that was John's home.

Hamish chided himself for not phoning first. He rapped on the door and waited while the rising gale whipped at his oilskin coat.

A small man opened the door and stared up at the tall policeman. 'I am Police Constable Hamish Macbeth from Lochdubh,' said Hamish. 'Might I be having a wee word with you?'

'Come in.'

Hamish followed him into a living room lined with books. A computer stood on a table by the window. Peat smouldered on the open fire. Over the fireplace hung a large framed photograph of the author accepting a plaque.

'You have interrupted my muse,' said John, and gave a great hee-haw sort of laugh.

He was only a little over five feet tall, be-spectacled, with thinning grey hair, the strands combed over a balding scalp. His eyes were large and brown above a squashy, open-pored nose and fleshy mouth. He wore a roll-necked brown sweater and brown cords.

'Sit down,' he said. 'You're making my neck ache.'

4

Hamish removed his cap and coiled his lanky length down into an armchair by the fire.

'Is that your own colour?' asked John, staring at Hamish's flaming-red hair.

'All my own. You don't seem to be surprised at getting a visit from the police.'

'I'm not married, my parents are dead and I have no close relatives. People are only frightened when they see a policeman at the door if they're worried about a loved one or have something to hide. So why have you come?'

'It's about your writing class.'

'I'll be delighted to see you there. You can pay for the whole term or at each class.'

'I wasn't thinking of attending. I don't think anyone will. They'll all be at home watching the telly.'

John looked a trifle smug. 'I have already had ten applications from the residents of Lochdubh.'

'Who might they be?'

'Ah.' John wagged a finger. 'I suggest you come along and see.'

'I might do that. Have you had much published?'

'I received the Tammerty Biscuit Award for Scottish literature.' John pointed to the photograph. 'That's me getting the award for my book *Tenement Days*. Have you read it?'

'No.'

'Then let me give you a copy.' John left the

5

room. Hamish looked around. A small table over against the wall opposite from the computer held the remains of a meal. Apart from the books lining the low walls and the large photograph over the fireplace, there were no ornaments or family photographs.

John came back in and handed him a copy of *Tenement Days*. 'I signed it,' he said. Hamish flipped it open and looked at the inscription. It read, 'To Hamish MacBeth. His first introduction to literature. John Heppel.'

'I haff read other books,' said Hamish crossly, the sudden sibilance of his highland accent showing he was annoyed. 'And my name is spelled without a capital B. What else have you written?'

'Oh, lots,' said John. 'I've just finished a film script for Strathbane Television.'

'What's it called?'

John looked suddenly uncomfortable. 'Well, it's a script for *Down in the Glen*.'

Hamish smiled. 'That's a soap.'

'But I have raised the tone, don't you see? To improve the public mind, even great authors such as myself must lower themselves to write for a popular series.'

'Indeed? Good luck to you. I had better be going.'

'Wait a bit. You asked about my work? I have been greatly influenced by the French authors such as Jean-Paul Sartre and François Mauriac. Even when I was at school, I became aware that I had a great gift. I was brought up in the mean streets of Glasgow, a hard environment for a sensitive boy. But I observed. I am a camera. I sometimes feel I have been sent down from another planet to observe.'

'Quite a lot of highland drunks feel the same way,' said Hamish, made malicious by boredom. 'You know, they all think they're off another planet.'

But John's eyes had taken on the self-obsessed glaze of the bore. 'You are wondering why I never married?'

'Last thing I was wondering,' muttered Hamish.

'There was one woman in my life, one great love. But she was married. We met in secret. Our passion soared like . . . like . . .'

'Buzzards?'

'The eagle,' corrected John crossly. 'She had raven hair and skin like milk.'

'Aye, well,' said Hamish, determinedly getting to his feet. 'All verra interesting, but I've got to go.'

'Oh, must you? Then I shall see you next Wednesday.'

Hamish jammed on his cap. 'Don't get up,' he said. 'I'll see myself out.'

He noticed that a wax coat hanging by the door was wet.

He was just getting into the Land Rover when John ran out after him. 'You've forgotten your book.'

7

'Aye, thanks.' Hamish took it from him and threw it on to the passenger seat and drove off at great speed.

He won't last the winter, he told himself, unaware at that time that John Heppel was to leave the Highlands but not in a way that Hamish Macbeth expected.

As Hamish drove along the waterfront in Lochdubh, he saw that one wire mesh waste bin had not yet been stolen by the fishermen to be used as a lobster pot. He stopped the Land Rover with a jerk, picked up John's book, opened the window, and hurled the book into the bin. The inscription had annoyed him.

He drove a little further and then noticed a small crowd outside Patel's general store. Mrs Wellington, the minister's wife, was one of the group, and she waved to him.

Hamish stopped again and rolled down the window. 'What's going on here?'

'It's dreadful,' said Mrs Wellington. 'Come and look.'

Hamish climbed down and walked over. The group parted to let him through. There on the whitewashed wall of the store by the door, someone had sprayed in red paint, 'Paki Go Home'.

'And he's not even Pakistani!' wailed Mrs Wellington. 'He's Indian.'

The door of the shop, which had been closed for the night, opened, and Mr Patel came out. 'Hamish, what's happened?' he asked.

'Some maniac's been writing on your walls,' said Hamish.

Mr Patel looked at the wall. 'Who would have done this?' he asked, looking round the little crowd.

'Do you sell spray paint?' asked Hamish.

'Yes, but never to children. I mean, I only sell it to people who're going to use it round the house.'

Hamish addressed the group. 'I want all of you to ask round the village and find out if anyone saw anybody near the shop. You closed half-day today, Mr Patel. It gets dark after two in the afternoon. So it must have happened sometime between then and now. In the meantime let's get some turpentine and wash the stuff off.'

'What about fingerprints?' asked Mrs Wellington.

'No forensic team's going to turn out for this, and the kit I've got wouldn't be able to get one off that wall. Let's get to it. And tell that new schoolteacher, Miss Garrety, that I'll be along to speak to the pupils tomorrow first thing.'

'You think it's children?' asked Angela Brodie, the doctor's wife, who had joined the group.

'I don't know,' said Hamish. 'I chust cannae think of anyone who would do this. Mr Patel is one of us and has been for ages.'

The group was getting larger, and everyone was desperate to take a hand at cleaning the wall. Hamish pushed back his cap and scratched his fiery hair. 'If it was "English Go Home", I could understand it,' he said to Angela. 'There's a lot of stupid English-bashing in Scotland these days.'

'But not in Lochdubh,' said Angela. 'It must be someone from outside. Everyone in Lochdubh knows that Mr Patel originally came from India.'

The next day Hamish put his odd-looking dog, Lugs, on the leash and walked along to the village school. The school, like his police station, was under threat. The children were taught up to the age of eleven years, and then the older ones were bussed to the secondary school in Strathbane. There had been various moves to close down the school, but each time the well-organized villagers had mounted such a strong protest that they had succeeded in keeping it.

Miss Freda Garrety, the schoolteacher, was a tiny slip of a thing in her twenties. She barely came up to Hamish's shoulder. She had straight black hair cut in a bob and a white triangular face with large black eyes. She was dressed in a black T-shirt and black trousers. Hamish thought she looked like a harlequin.

'I'm here to speak to your pupils,' said Hamish.

'About the graffiti?' She had a lowland accent. 'Make it quick. Exams are coming up.'

Hamish walked into the classroom, where the children still sat behind old-fashioned desks: the oldest at the back and the youngest at the front.

He walked to the front of the room. 'I'm here to talk to you about the racist graffiti on the wall of the general store. This is a disgrace and should not be allowed to happen in Lochdubh. Do any of you know anything about this?'

Solemn faces stared back at him, but nobody spoke. 'Now, some of you may know something but don't want to tell me in front of the others. If you do know anything at all, I want you to call at the police station with one of your parents.'

A small boy put his hand up.

'Yes?'

'My faither says there's too many foreigners in this country. Maybe you should speak to him.'

'You're Dermott Taggart, am I right?'

'Yes.'

'Is your father at home?'

'He's down on a building site in Strathbane.'

'Do you think he might have had something to do with this?'

11

Dermott looked suddenly frightened. 'Don't be telling him I said anything,' he said, and burst into tears. Freda rushed forward to comfort him.

'Anyone else?' asked Hamish.

Silence.

'Well, listen carefully. Racism is a serious crime. The culprit will be punished, and mark my words, I'll find out who did this.'

Hamish returned to the police station and went into his office, where he stared blankly at the computer. Who on earth would want to paint a racist slogan on Patel's shop?

There was a cry from the kitchen door. 'Hamish, the telly's here. They're outside Patel's wi' that writer cheil.'

Hamish rushed out. Archie Maclean stood there. 'Ye wouldnae think they'd bother.'

Hamish walked with him round to Patel's. John Heppel was standing outside the shop, facing a camera crew.

'. . . and that is all I have to say,' he was declaring pompously. 'I, John Heppel, will do my utmost to help the police find the perpetrator of this wicked crime. Thank you.'

Hamish's hazel eyes narrowed in suspicion. John Heppel was made up for the cameras, and yet he could not see a make-up girl anywhere around.

He pushed his way through the crowd that had gathered to where John was talking with the interviewer, a pretty girl called Jessma Gardener.

'How did you find out about this?' demanded Hamish of John.

'Ah, Constable. I just happened to be passing and saw the television crew.'

Hamish leaned forward and drew a long finger down John's cheek and then studied the brown make-up on his finger.

'Do you usually wear make-up?' he asked.

John flushed angrily. 'I am so used to television appearances,' he said, 'that I carry a kit in the car. I owe it to my readers to look my best at all times.'

Hamish turned to Jessma. 'How did *you* hear about this?'

'Someone phoned the news desk late last night.'

'Would you mind phoning up and asking the name of whoever it was phoned the story in?'

'I've got to be going,' said John, and he pushed his way past Hamish and through the crowd.

While Jessma took out her mobile and phoned, Hamish stood watching the retreat of John Heppel.

When she rang off, she said, 'It was an anonymous caller. Then John phoned and said he would be at the shop. As he's writing a script for one of our shows, we thought we may as well interview him. Me, I think it's a waste of time. You should have heard the whole speech. You'd think the wee mannie ran the Highlands. It'll probably end up in the bin.'

Hamish went back to the police station, collected his dog, and drove off in the Land Rover in the direction of Cnothan. He put the light on the roof and turned on the siren as Lugs, his dog, rolled his odd blue eyes at his master. Lugs hated that siren.

Hamish cut off several miles to Cnothan by bumping along a croft track and arrived at John Heppel's house before the writer.

He got down from the car and waited.

He searched through the rubbish bin at the side of the house and was still searching when John drove up.

'What are you doing?' demanded the writer angrily.

Hamish straightened up. 'I was looking for a can of spray paint.'

'I'll sue you for defamation of character.'

'You do that and I'll get a warrant to search your house and examine your clothes for paint. I think you sprayed that graffiti to get yourself a bit of publicity.'

'How dare you!'

'I've got enough on my plate at the moment without bothering about a silly man like you. Don't ever do anything like that again.'

14

'I'm telling you, I'll sue you!'

'Go ahead,' said Hamish. 'I'd enjoy seeing the sort of publicity that would get you. When I arrived at your place last night, your coat was still wet. You'd been out. Any more publicity stunts like that and I'll have you.'

'I hate that sort of person,' said Hamish to his dog as he drove off. 'Now, what do I do, Lugs? Do I tell the villagers? Och, it's chust a storm in a teacup. He won't try anything like that again. But I will have a word on the quiet with Mr Patel.'

Mr Patel's eyebrows shot up into his hair when Hamish took him outside his shop and quietly explained his suspicions about the writer.

'Are ye sure?' asked Mr Patel. 'I've signed up for one o' his classes.'

'You want to be a writer?' asked Hamish, momentarily diverted. 'What kind of book?'

'I was thinking I might write my life story. You know, how I started off selling stuff out o' a suitcase round the Hebrides until I had enough to start a shop.' His brown eyes took on a dreamy, unfocussed look. 'I'll call it *An Indian's Life in the Far North of Scotland*.'

'Maybe you should try for something snappier.'

'Like what?'

'Cannae think of anything.'

'There you are! That's why I need to go to a writing class.'

'Anyway,' said Hamish, 'I've no actual proof he did it, and in order to prove it, I'd need a warrant to search his house and I can't see me getting it. So we'll keep this between ourselves.'

'So you're not sure he did it?'

'Pretty certain. I mean, he turned up with make-up on.'

'Maybe he's . . . well, you know . . . that way inclined.'

'He's inclined to getting his stupid face on television, that's all.'

'Hey, Hamish!'

Hamish turned round. Callum McSween, the dustman, stood there. 'I found a book inscribed to you in the bin. Here it is.'

'Oh, thanks,' mumbled Hamish. He wanted to say he had put it there deliberately but suddenly wanted to forget all about John Heppel.

He nodded goodbye to both of them. He drove to the police station, got down, and helped Lugs out because the dog's legs were too short to enable him to jump down from the Land Rover. He looked at the book in his hand.

He glanced along the waterfront. It was now the dinner hour – Lochdubh residents still took dinner in the middle of the day – and the waterfront was deserted.

16

He hurled the book so hard that it flew straight across the waterfront and over the sea wall.

Hamish was just frying some chops when there was a knock at the kitchen door. The locals never came to the front door. He opened it. In the days when Hamish was a police sergeant, his caller, Clarry Graham, had worked for him – or, rather, had not worked, Clarry finding that his talents lay in being a chef.

To Hamish's dismay, he was clutching That Book.

'It's quiet up at the Tommel Castle Hotel at the moment,' said Clarry plaintively. 'I was out fishing in the loch when this book fell out o' the sky and right into my boat. It's inscribed to you.'

'Thanks,' said Hamish.

'Must've been kids,' said Clarry.

'Come in.'

'You don't want to be reading something like that anyway,' said Clarry. 'Full o' nasty words. I'm telling you, there's an eff in every line.'

'That's the fellow who's going to be giving those writing classes.'

'Oh, I'd signed up for those.'

'You, Clarry? A book? I mean, what about?'

'I'm going to call it *From Police Station to Kitchen*.'

'Look, Clarry, it iss awfy hard to get a book published these days. Particularly a life story. You really have to be some kind o' celebrity. Besides, this John Heppel seems to write the sort of stuff you wouldn't want to read.'

'He's going to tell us about publishers and agents,' said Clarry stubbornly. 'I'd like to make a bit o' money. Just look at what J.K. Rowling earns.'

'Didn't it dawn on you that J.K. Rowling can *write*? Clarry, only four and a half per cent of the authors in this world can afford to support themselves. I 'member reading that.'

Clarry's round face took on a mulish look, and Hamish suppressed a sigh. Clarry obviously thought he was destined to be one of the four and a half per cent.

When Clarry had left, Hamish began to think uneasily about John's writing classes. John, he was beginning to feel, was some sort of dangerous foreign body introduced into the highland system.

He decided to attend the first class. It would upset John to see him there, and Hamish looked forward to upsetting John. He flicked open John's book and began to read. It was one of those pseudo-literary stream-of-consciousness books set in the slums of Glasgow. The 'grittiness' was supplied by four-letter words. The anti-hero was a druggie whose favourite occupation seemed to be slashing with a broken bottle anyone in a pub who looked at him the wrong way. The heroine put up with all this with loving kindness. Hamish flicked to the end of the book, where a reformed anti-hero was preaching to the youth of Glasgow. No one could accuse the book of being plot-driven. Hackneyed similes and metaphors clunked their way through the thick volume.

Maybe it was all right, he thought ruefully. Like all Highlanders, he was quick to take offence and loathed being patronized. The inscription still rankled, however.

There was another knock at the door, very faint. Hamish opened it and looked down at Dermott Taggart, the small boy who had thought his father might be responsible for the graffiti.

'Come ben,' said Hamish. Then he cursed. Black smoke was rising from the frying pan. He'd forgotten about the chops.

'Sit down, laddie,' he said over his shoulder. 'I'll just put this mess in the bin. I havenae any soft drinks, but I could make you some tea.'

'I don't want anything,' said the boy in a whisper.

Hamish got rid of the chops. 'Sit,' he ordered. 'You didn't really think your da was responsible for the graffiti?'

Dermott hung his head.

'I think,' said Hamish gently, 'that something at home is bothering you. I think you want a policeman to call. What's going on at home?'

The child began to cry. Hamish fished a box of tissues out of a cupboard and handed it to him, then waited patiently.

At last the crying ended on a hiccupping sob. 'Dad's hitting Ma,' he choked out.

'Does he drink?'

'A lot.'

'It's hard for me to do anything unless your mother puts in a complaint.'

'You won't tell the Social?' gasped the boy in sudden alarm.

'No, I won't do that,' said Hamish, knowing that no matter how bad the parents, abused children still lived in terror of being snatched from their homes by the Social Services. 'Leave it with me. I'll think of something.'

When the boy had gone, Hamish turned over in his mind what he knew about the boy's father. Alistair Taggart took occasional building jobs down in Strathbane. Hamish couldn't remember seeing him drinking in the village pub. Perhaps he did his drinking in Strathbane and drove home.

He was almost relieved to have an ordinary, if unpleasant, village problem to cope with instead of fretting that John Heppel would somehow bring trouble to the area.

Chapter Two

O! he's as tedious
As a tired horse, a railing wife;
Worse than a smoky house. I had rather live
With cheese and garlic in a windmill far,
Than feed on cates and have him talk to me
In any summer house in Christendom.
                    – William Shakespeare

It was one of those odd spring-like November days you occasionally get in the Highlands where a balmy wind blows in off the Gulf Stream. Hamish longed to go fishing, but Wednesday had come around, the evening of John's first class, and he had not yet dealt with Dermott's problem.

He found out which building site Alistair Taggart had been working on, phoned, and found he had been laid off. He set out for the Taggart cottage, which was at the end of the village where a large hotel had once operated and now stood empty.

Taggart's wife, Maisie, answered the door.

21

She put a hand to her throat when she saw him. 'What is it, Hamish? Not my boy?'

'No, no,' he said soothingly. 'I'm asking everyone in the village if they saw anyone put that graffiti on Patel's wall.'

Maisie Taggart had the faded remains about her of what had once been a pretty woman. There was an ugly bruise on one cheek.

'Who is it?' shouted a man's voice. 'Another of your fancy men?'

'That will be your man,' said Hamish equably. 'I'll speak to him.'

She looked frightened and flustered. 'Now's no' the good time.' And then she was thrust aside, and Alistair loomed in the doorway.

'What is it?' he barked. 'I'm just sorting this bitch out.' He jerked a thumb at his quivering wife. 'She says she's going to thon writing class. Wasting my good money so she can see her fancy man.'

Maisie squeezed past her belligerent husband and disappeared inside the house.

'And you can get lost!' shouted Alistair.

'I was chust calling to ask you if you knew anything about the graffiti on Patel's shop, but now I'm here, you and I are going to have a serious talk.'

Alistair made to slam the door, but Hamish put a hand on his arm and hooked him out on to the waterfront.

'If you hit me,' said Hamish, 'you will be charged with assault and go to prison.'

Alistair dropped the fists he had raised and then demanded, 'Well, whit?'

'You cannae keep things quiet in a wee village like this,' lied Hamish, reflecting that Alistair's abuse of his wife had been kept amazingly secret. 'We all know you beat your wife.'

'Who's saying so?'

'Everyone. She's got a bruise on her cheek.'

'Fell down the stairs.'

'Aw, pull the other one. That excuse is as old as the hills. I'm after you now, Alistair Taggart. Your wife is going to that writing class. Every time now you threaten her, I'll probably be outside your house with a tape recorder. When you drive back from Strathbane, if you get another job, the traffic cops will be looking for you and they'll check you for drunk driving. Now, let's just take a look at that car of yours and your papers.'

'This is harassment!'

'It'll do you no harm to get a taste of what your wife's been suffering.' Hamish walked over to where Alistair's car was parked at the side of his cottage. 'Let me see. The front nearside tyre needs to be replaced. Keys?'

Alistair handed them over and waited, sweating in the balmy air as Hamish did a thorough check of car and papers. 'You need new brake lights,' said Hamish finally, 'and your tax disc is out o' date.'

The bully in Alistair crumbled. 'Look,' he wheedled, 'I'll take Maisie to that class maself and treat her nice. Will you leave me alone then?'

'Probably,' said Hamish. 'After you fix your car. Behave yourself.'

Hamish returned to the police station and then set out to patrol his extensive highland beat with Lugs beside him. He had given up leaving Lugs with Angela, the doctor's wife, because she had complained that Lugs spent more time with her than he did at home.

Lugs was a thoroughly spoilt animal. Hamish sometimes still had a pang when he thought of the death of his old dog, Towser, wondering if he had treated the animal well, wondering if he could have done something, anything, to prolong Towser's life, and clever Lugs was the beneficiary. He was a greedy dog and could easily stop the diets Hamish tried to put him on by lying down and closing his eyes and whimpering.

As Lugs sat beside Hamish with his large ears flopping and something that looked remarkably like a human grin on his face, Hamish felt, not for the first time, that he was saddled with some sort of possessive wife.

A new pub had opened out on the Lochdubh–Strathbane road called Dimity Dan's. Hamish had visited it several times since its grand opening a month before. On the first night there had been a stabbing. He suspected the owner, Dan Buffort, of supplying drugs.

The youth of the Highlands who once left for the cities or the army as soon as they had graduated from school or college, now showed a distressing propensity to stay at home in the villages and slope around, making trouble.

Hamish entered the smoky pub. Two youths were playing snooker, others were propping up the bar drinking Bacardi Breezers. A lot of alcopops, those sweet alcoholic drinks, were lined up behind the bar. The manufacturers had claimed that they weren't targeting young people with their products, but Hamish did not believe a word of it. They were produced in tempting little innocuous-looking bottles with names like Archers Aqua Peach, Bliss, and Mike's Hard Lemonade.

Hamish ordered a mineral water. 'I hope you aren't selling to under-age girls and boys,' he said.

Dan Buffort was a burly man with thick tattooed arms, ginger hair and small piggy eyes.

'Wouldnae dream o' it,' he said with a grin.

'I've heard otherwise,' said Hamish. 'If I catch you just the once, you'll lose your licence.'

'I've naethin' tae fear.' Dan polished another glass.

Something was nagging at the back of Hamish's mind. When he had driven up to the pub, he was sure he had noticed something different. He paid for his mineral water and hurried out of the pub. He stood back from the building and stared up at it.

And then he saw it.

A new CCTV camera had been installed, but instead of pointing down to the pub entrance and the car park, it was pointing directly along the Lochdubh Road.

Hamish ran back into the pub and through to the toilets. A window was open. He looked out, and there, racing over the moors in the distance, were two small figures.

He went back into the bar and confronted Dan. 'You will get that new camera of yours pointed down at the entrance where it should be. You put it there so you'd know when I was coming.'

'It was those idiots who installed it,' said Dan, quite unfazed. 'I'll get it put right.'

'See that you do. I'll be watching you closely from now on, day and night. One sight of an under-age boy or girl or one sight or suspicion of drugs and I'll have you closed down fast.'

Hamish left and continued on his long beat. His duties involved calling in on the elderly and the isolated, and he got back to the police station just in time to change into civilian clothes and attend John Heppel's meeting at the village hall.

26

There were a lot of villagers there. Twin sisters, Jessie and Nessie Currie, were in the front row beside Mrs Wellington and Archie Maclean. Clarry was in the row behind them, and beside him was Willie Lamont, another ex-policeman who had gone into the restaurant business, Mr Patel, Callum McSween and Freda, the schoolteacher. Various other villagers filled the other seats. To Hamish's surprise, Alistair Taggart was there with his wife, Maisie.

Hamish took a seat at the back next to Angela Brodie, the doctor's wife. 'I'm surprised to see you here,' he said. 'Don't you know the man's an idiot?'

'Well, he got a book published. I've always wanted to write. I need all the help I can get. Where is he? We were due to start at seven-thirty.'

'He'll want to make an entrance,' said Hamish.

At quarter to eight precisely, John Heppel strode into the room. His coat was slung over his shoulders and he was carrying a large travelling bag. He hung his coat on a hook and then mounted the stage, carrying the bag, and faced the class. He was dressed all in black: black roll-necked sweater, black cords and black shoes. His face was made up.

'He has the make-up on, make-up on,' hissed Jessie Currie, who, like Browning's thrush, said everything twice over.

27

'Maybe he's a transferite,' said Willie Lamont.

'*Transvestite* is what you mean,' boomed Mrs Wellington.

'I have put on my television make-up because they said they would be here,' said John crossly. 'Perhaps we should wait.'

'I cannae wait all nicht,' called out Archie. 'I've the fishing to go to.'

There was a murmur of agreement.

'Very well,' said John. He bent down and opened the bag and lifted a pile of his books on to the table in front of him. 'At the end of the class I will be glad to sign one of my books for you. A special price. Ten pounds.'

'Ten pounds!' exclaimed someone. 'They're remaindered for three pounds ninety down at Best Books in Strathbane.'

John ignored the interruption.

'I will tell you all how I got started,' he began. His eyes assumed a fixed look, and his voice took on the droning note of the habitual bore. 'I was born into one of the worst slums in Glasgow. We didn't even have a bath.'

Hamish's mind drifted off as the voice went inexorably on, and he only snapped to attention after twenty minutes when Mrs Wellington stood up and said, 'You said you would teach us how to write.'

John looked flustered. 'I think, then,' he said, 'we will start by discussing the novel. Perhaps we will discuss linear progression.'

'Do you mean the plot?' called Hamish.

'Er, yes.'

'Then why not say so?'

'I tell you what I am going to do,' said John. 'I am going to ask you all to bring a piece of writing here next week. It can be anything you like – poetry, essays, fiction, anything – and I will give you the benefit of my expert advice. It will be easier for me to assess your work if it is typed and in double spacing.'

'You mean we've all got to get computers, get computers?' wailed Jessie.

'Perhaps not right away,' said John. 'I will now take questions.'

Archie piped up. 'Have you met J.K. Rowling?'

'Ah, yes, a most charming lady. We signed books together in Edinburgh. She was kind enough to congratulate me on my work.'

What a liar, thought Hamish. Any bookshop lucky enough to get J.K. Rowling was not going to clutter up the premises with a minor author.

'Do you think it's easier to write for children?' asked Mrs Wellington.

'Very much so,' said John.

Angela stood up, her thin face flushed with annoyance. 'I think that is very misleading,' she said. 'A lot of people are misguided enough to think that writing a children's book is easy, but the author needs to have a talent for that genre.'

'Perhaps I said that,' conceded John, 'because I personally would find it easy despite my own unfortunate childhood. Why, I remember one dark Christmas . . .'

And he was off again down memory lane. A bored highland audience does not stamp out or make any noise. It just melts away. Hamish decided to join them.

He was just heading back to the police station when he saw the Strathbane Television van approaching along the waterfront. He stood out in the middle of the road and held up his hand.

Jessma Gardener was in the front seat. She rolled down the window. 'If you're on your way to the writing class, you're too late,' said Hamish. 'It's finished.'

'Oh, good,' said Jessma. 'I couldn't bear the thought of it. But the lights are still on in the village hall.'

'Cleaning up,' lied Hamish, who well knew that some of the audience were still there. 'Why does Strathbane News want to cover a village writing class?'

'There's a new drama executive who handles the soap. John's written a script for it. The exec says it's brilliant, so we're asked to cover anything John Heppel wants us to. Still, thank goodness for an early evening.'

She waved to him. The van did a U-turn and headed back out of the village.

'I've been very petty,' Hamish told his dog when he entered the police station. 'I should have let the wee man have his bit of glory, and him all made up for it. But I don't like him and that's a fact. It's not because he's a bore. It's something else. I feel he means trouble.'

'Do you usually talk to your dog?' asked a voice behind him.

Hamish blushed and turned round.

Freda Garrety stood there, smiling. Hamish had left the kitchen door open.

'Can I help you?' he asked stiffly.

'I wanted to talk to you about John Heppel.'

'All right. Shut the door and sit down. Tea or something stronger?'

'I wouldn't mind a dram.'

Hamish took down a nearly full whisky bottle from the cupboard and two glasses.

'That's a very odd-looking dog,' she said. 'I've never seen a dog with such blue eyes.'

'Water?' asked Hamish, ignoring her remark because he was cross with her for finding him talking to Lugs.

'Just a little.'

Hamish filled a jug with water and put it along with the whisky and glasses on the table. He poured two measures.

Freda added a little water to her glass. 'He presented a copy of his book to the school library. Because he'd won a literary prize and all that, I didn't think of checking it. Then I found one child after another was asking to borrow it. So I took it home and read it. It's full of swear-words and explicit sex. Now, I know they get a lot of stuff on television and on the Internet these days, but I do try to keep them children as long as possible. I mean, I don't want to contribute to fouling up their minds.'

Hamish shared her worry. Despite all the encroachments of the modern world, there was still a certain innocence about the village children which had been taken away from their counterparts in the cities.

Again he had a feeling that John Heppel was a cancer eating into local society.

Freda spoke again. 'A lot of the parents are furious, but then there are others who are seduced by the idea that they, too, could write a book. They say John's book is literature and there are a lot of nasty things in Shakespeare.'

'I think we're worrying ower-much,' said Hamish slowly. 'He's so self-obsessed, so conceited, and so boring that people will stop attending his classes. This will hurt his vanity. I think he moved here to be a big fish in a small pond. Once the locals have got over the romance of writing, they'll ignore him and he won't be able to bear that. What made *you* decide to come here?'

'I was working in a comprehensive in Lanarkshire. The kids' parents were mostly on the dole. It was a miserable existence. Some of the boys were violent. One day one of them held a knife to my throat in the playground.

He was overpowered by two of the masters. The school tried to suspend him, but the bleeding hearts at the education authority decided he had to stay. I saw the job up here advertised. I love it. I love the children.'

'It's a lonely life for a young woman.'

'Oh, on my weekends off I go clubbing in Inverness.'

Hamish suddenly felt ancient. How old was she? Hard to tell with her neat harlequin features.

'I have never been clubbing,' he said.

'You can come with me one weekend, if you like.'

'That would be grand,' said Hamish. 'I like new experiences. More whisky?'

'No, I've got exam papers to correct. Let's just hope John Heppel fades away.'

Despite the boredom of Heppel's initial class, most who had attended were determined to write.

Archie Maclean, banished from home as usual by his house-proud wife, was sitting on the waterfront wall, busy scribbling in a large notebook.

Hamish called at the manse to see if the normally sensible Mrs Wellington had given up the idea of writing, only to find her seated at her kitchen table in front of an old

Remington typewriter, bashing away energetically at the keys.

'What is it, Hamish?' she asked crossly. He had walked in by the open door, the weather being still unseasonably warm.

'I'm disappointed in you,' said Hamish. 'You don't really think that scunner can do anything to help?'

'I've always wanted to write. I'm starting with something easy. I am going to prostitute myself by writing one of those little romances.'

Hamish sighed. 'I once spoke to a writer who said you can't write down, and if you don't enjoy reading romances, then you can't write them.'

'That's where you're wrong,' said Mrs Wellington triumphantly. 'I am getting along just fine.'

Then she ignored him and began to rattle the keys busily.

Hamish left, wondering whether he was being a killjoy. Surely it was better for the villagers to exercise their minds during the long winter months than sit every evening watching television.

He walked out and down from the manse. A Strathbane Electrics van was parked on the waterfront, and two men seemed to be busy delivering computers.

He shook his head. 'It'll all end in tears.'

'Talking to yourself, Hamish? That's a bad sign.'

Hamish turned round. Angela Brodie was standing there, smiling up at him, her wispy hair blowing about her face.

'I've still got a nagging worry about Heppel.'

'He's an awful bore,' said Angela. 'But it's all turned out a bit of fun. It's a long time since Lochdubh's been so excited about anything.'

'But a lot of people left the class before he had finished.'

'It's because he said he would look at their work. Once they all got home, they began to dream about bestseller lists.'

'I think a lot of them'll be getting nervous breakdowns before they grasp how to operate a computer.'

'Ah, that's where you're wrong. I heard Jessie Currie saying that Hamish Macbeth had a computer at the police station, so he could help them.'

Hamish stared at her in alarm. 'I'd best be off on my beat.'

He hurried back to the police station, collected Lugs, and got into the Land Rover.

The mountains were shrouded in mist as he drove up into the moors and foothills. The narrow single-track road shone black in front of him. Then as he reached the crest of the hill above Lochdubh, the mist began to roll up the mountains. He stopped the car and watched. This, he reflected, was one of the reasons he loved this part of the world so much. It was like watching a curtain rise at the theatre. Up and up went the mist, a stiff wind sprang up, and then the sky above the mountains cleared to pale blue, the sun shone out, and the wet road in front of him turned to gold.

He got out of the car and lifted Lugs down. The dog scampered off into the heather. Hamish stood with his hands on his hips, surveying the scene. He turned round and looked back down to Lochdubh. On the other side of the loch, in front of the dark green of the fir plantation, a perfect rainbow curved down into the still black waters of the loch. As he watched, the rainbow faded and the loch changed to deep blue.

He gave a sigh of satisfaction. He could feel all his troubles about John Heppel rolling up and away from him like the mist.

He was sure his fears about the man bringing something bad into the area were wrong.

And that feeling lasted until something prompted him to attend the next writing class.

Chapter Three

At last it grew, and grew, and bore and bore,
Till at length
It grew a gallows

— Thomas Kyd

Hamish had not planned to visit the writing class on the following Wednesday, but Angela and Dr Brodie said if he would come along they would take him for dinner to the Italian restaurant afterwards. Dr Brodie said Angela had written a very good story, and he wanted to see how she got on.

The village hall was as full as it had been the week before. Hands clutched manuscripts. Faces were flushed with excitement.

As usual, John made a late entrance. He began, 'There was another part of my life which influenced my writing. It all began . . .'

'No!' shouted Mrs Wellington, formidable in tweed and a large felt hat with a pheasant's feather thrust through it. 'You said you would look at our work. There's a lot of us here. Let's get started.'

'Oh, very well,' said John sulkily. 'Who's first?'

There was silence, everyone suddenly being struck with shyness.

'I'll start,' said Mrs Wellington. She lumbered up to the stage on her stout brogues. 'I have started writing one of those little romances. Beneath my intelligence, but it's a beginning. I've done one chapter.'

John's mobile phone rang. Hamish noticed that once more he was made up. He heard John saying, 'But you promised!' Then he lowered his voice and snarled something before ringing off.

Strathbane Television is not coming, thought Hamish. And he's in a right fury about it.

'Read out some of your work,' John ordered.

Mrs Wellington shifted her large feet uncomfortably. 'I would rather you read some of it yourself.'

To her dismay, he began to read out loud. 'It was a dreich day in the glen when Claribell McWhirter went out to feed the hens. Her long red hair blew about her white shoulders . . .

'Was she naked?' sneered John.

'Of course not.'

'Then how does the reader know she has white shoulders?'

'She's wearing one of those . . . one of those Gypsy blouses, off the shoulder.'

38

'You should have said so. Now to her name. Claribell is the name of a cow, my dear woman. Hardly romantic.'

'I can change that.'

He flicked through the pages. 'If I were you, I would buy some romances and get some idea of what to write. This is rubbish. Next?'

Mrs Wellington, her face flaming with fury, grabbed her manuscript and clumped off the stage.

A thin youth walked up to the stage. Hamish recognized Angus Petrie, a forestry worker. 'It's science fiction,' said Angus proudly. 'I've only got the first few pages, but it'll give you an idea.'

'Read!' ordered John.

Angus went as red as his hair and pimples, but he gamely cleared his throat and began: 'The five suns were setting over the planet Zog when Burt Lightheart walked back to his cave followed by his trusty gorg, Siegfried.'

'What's a gorg?' interrupted John.

'It's a hairy creature which lives on the planet, rather like a pig.'

'Might have been a good idea to tell us that. And why the hell would he call this gorg Siegfried? Fans of Wagner up there, are they? Oh, go on, go on.'

'His wife, Zelda, had prepared him a suc- culent supper of forret's flesh.'

'What's a forret?'

'It's a ferret what's had it,' shouted someone, and was immediately shushed.

'It's a big hairy thing, rather like a mastodon,' said Angus.

'But we don't know that because you haven't told us.'

'Gie the lad a chance,' shouted Archie.

'I'm not reading any more,' said Angus stiffly, and walked off the stage.

And so it went on, with one would-be writer after another being crushed. The Currie sisters were particularly incensed at being told their offering read like an immature school essay. Alistair Taggart was told his story was incomprehensible because he had written it in Gaelic, and he was only allowed to read a few sentences. He looked for a moment as if he was going to strike John.

And then it was Angela Brodie's turn. Her husband had insisted. She began to read in a quavering voice, and then her voice grew more confident as she read on. It was a short story about a newcomer trying to come to terms with life in the far north of Scotland. The hall was completely silent, everyone becoming wrapped up in the story.

John sat biting his knuckles. He's desperately trying to find something to criticize, thought Hamish.

When Angela finished, there was a burst of applause. 'Shows promise,' said John sourly.

'But you've got a long way to go before you can consider yourself a writer.'

Archie Maclean leapt to his feet. 'No,' he shouted, 'thon was grand, and you're the one that's got one lang way tae go afore you can consider yourself a writer.'

There were cries of agreement.

'The class is over,' said John. 'I will see what progress you have made next week.'

He strode from the stage, hitched his coat down from a peg, swung it round his shoulders, and left with an angry banging of the door.

Hamish looked around the hall at the furious faces, at the disappointed faces, and at the hurt faces. Being highland himself, he knew that a good lot of them would be plotting revenge.

He left the hall and returned to the police station and got into the Land Rover. It was time to have a serious talk with John Heppel.

The night was clear and starry, the air was more seasonably cold. He drove up the rutted track to John's croft house crouching under the thick branches of a large oak tree. Apart from the forestry plantations, there were very few trees in Sutherland because of the ferocious gales. To ward off fairies, there were rowan trees growing outside cottage doors, but this great oak tree was unusual.

41

Hamish knocked on the door. When John answered it, he stared up at Hamish and scowled. 'What now?'

'It iss about your behaviour this evening,' said Hamish. John did not know Hamish well enough to be alarmed at the sudden sibilance of the policeman's accent – a sign that Hamish was seriously upset. 'How dare you humiliate folks so badly? Who the hell do you think you are, you with your rotten manners? I want you to write letters of apology to the members of your class and return their money. How much was the fee? Ten pounds? You are a fraud. You were supposed to be teaching them how to write, not demoralizing them.'

'I am a literary writer,' spluttered John. 'I have my standards. I –'

'I should ha' never let that business about the graffiti go,' said Hamish. 'In fact, I'm taking the matter to Strathbane. They take racial insults very seriously these days. I'll have you out of Cnothan if it's the last thing I do. Now, are you going to write these letters?'

'Bugger off.'

'Well, you asked for it.'

Hamish turned on his heel. As he walked to the Land Rover, he heard the door bang angrily behind him.

He was worried. He knew Lochdubh would never forgive John. In fact, he was so worried he forgot he had promised to have dinner with Angela and her husband.

* * *

The next day he was about to go out on his beat, late as usual, when he saw the Strathbane Television van parked on the waterfront and Jessma Gardener interviewing Mrs Wellington, who was surrounded by members of the writing class.

Hamish walked forward to listen.

'John Heppel is a fraud and a charlatan,' boomed Mrs Wellington while the soundman struggled frantically to mute her voice. 'He deliberately set out to shame all of us, one by one. A lot of us showed promise, but I don't think any of us will have the courage to write again.'

Jessie and Nessie Currie pushed forward. 'We'd written an awfy nice story, "From Our Kitchen Window", and he just sneered at us,' said Nessie, 'after I'd read only a few words. Then there's the money we spent on a computer.'

'On a computer,' echoed the Greek chorus that was her sister.

'And I think we should be getting our money back.'

There was a cry of approval.

'Here comes the wee man,' shouted a voice from the back of the crowd.

John Heppel drove up. I wonder how he knew the television people were here, thought Hamish. Or does he smell out publicity the way a wasp can smell jam?

'Mr Heppel,' said Jessma. 'It seems your writing class wants their money back.'

John did not have make-up on, but he had browned his face with fake tan.

He took up a position in front of the camera. He cleared his throat. 'One must be cruel to be kind,' he said pompously. 'The shelves of bookshops are already overcrowded with books which should never have been published.'

'Like yours, you dirty wee man,' shouted Alistair Taggart. 'I'll get you if it's the last thing I do.'

John spread his chubby hands in a placatory gesture. 'You are all suffering from wounded ego. You . . .'

From the back of the crowd, a well-aimed tomato sailed over heads and landed right on John's face. The villagers cheered. The tomato was followed by an egg. Other missiles sailed through the air. 'Stop filming!' howled John, dodging right and left, but the camera rolled on. He saw Hamish and shouted, 'You're condoning this!'

'All right, that's enough,' said Hamish reluctantly.

John rounded on Jessma. 'Harry Tarrant, your boss, is a friend of mine. I'll get him to sack you.'

'He's the drama executive,' said Jessma. 'I work for news.'

John strode off to his car, staggering slightly

as Archie Maclean landed a kick on his bottom.

Jessma turned to Hamish. 'We've got good stuff here. Watch the news at six.'

'How did you hear about the class?' asked Hamish.

'Six of your villagers phoned in last night with complaints.'

'Won't you get in trouble with this drama executive he was talking about?'

'No. He might shout and complain, but we can say we can't consult the drama department over news.'

'Let's hope that's the end of John,' said Hamish. 'I'll be right glad to see the back of that man.'

The wind had shifted round to the north and was blowing with increasing ferocity. The crowd began to scatter, people huddling coats around themselves.

Hamish set off on his beat. He decided to call in at the Tommel Castle Hotel. The hotel had once been the home of the love of his life, Priscilla Halburton-Smythe, until her father had fallen on hard times and had turned the place into a successful hotel.

Hamish wanted to hear if there was any news about Priscilla. He knew she had planned to get married and that the wedding kept getting postponed, and although he told himself he was no longer interested in her, his heart rose at each postponement.

Mr Johnson, the manager, came out to greet him. 'Mooching coffee as usual, Hamish?'

'No, but if you've got any, I'd like a cup.'

'Come into the office.'

Hamish followed him in with Lugs at his heels. 'That dog of yours is too fat,' said Mr Johnson.

'He's chust fine,' said Hamish, irritated, while mentally promising to put Lugs on yet another diet.

Mr Johnson poured him a cup of coffee. 'What brings you?'

'You forget. The hotel's on my beat. I'm supposed to check up that you aren't harbouring terrorists or running drugs.'

'You need to check on Dimity Dan's for drugs.'

'You've heard something?'

'Just a buzz here and there. Priscilla's not married, if that's why you really came.'

Hamish's face flamed as red as his hair. 'This was supposed to be a friendly call,' he said stiffly.

'Well, sit down and stop glaring at me. What's all this about John Heppel creating mayhem in Lochdubh? One of the maids said there was quite a scene on the waterfront.'

Hamish told him about the writing class. 'That's a shame,' said Mr Johnson. 'We've got a writer staying here, Mary Timper. You know, she writes family sagas. Very popular.'

'Any chance of meeting her?'

'Why?'

'I just had this idea that maybe I could get her to talk to the folks who'd written stuff, and get a proper opinion from her.'

'I suppose it'll do no harm if you ask her.' He picked up the phone and dialled a number. 'Miss Timper. There's someone down here would like a word with you. It's our local bobby. No, no, nothing serious. He wants to ask your help. Right. He'll be in the lounge.' He replaced the phone. 'She'll be right down. Take yourself off to the lounge and leave that dog of yours here.'

Left alone, Lugs sadly eyed the closed door through which his master had just left. Then he sniffed the air. Biscuits! Mr Johnson had left a plate of biscuits on his desk beside the coffee cups.

He stood up on his hind legs and felt with his forepaws. Then he climbed up on Mr Johnson's chair. He chomped his way through the whole plate of biscuits and then tried to slurp the coffee out of the manager's cup, but it tipped over and the contents spilled across the desk.

Somewhere in Lugs's doggy brain, he sensed he was now in trouble. He climbed down from the chair and sat near the door. A maid opened the door. Lugs darted past her and ran out to the Land Rover and lay down on the far side of it.

In the meantime Hamish was shaking hands with Mary Timper. She was a pleasant, grey-haired motherly-looking woman with pale blue eyes magnified by large glasses.

'What brings you to Sutherland?' asked Hamish.

'I came because of the hotel's reputation. I like hotels. I like someone else to do the cooking and housecleaning once in a while. But you didn't call to ask me why I'm here, did you?'

'No. We've got a writing class in Lochdubh.'

'Ah, yes, someone called John Heppel. I haven't read him.'

'You wouldn't want to. It's like this.' Hamish told her about the humiliation of the villagers and ended with, 'So I just wondered if maybe you could look at their work and give them all a bit of a boost.'

She sighed. 'I'm not an editor.'

'You see,' pleaded Hamish, 'some of the folks bought computers, and they were all so excited about the writing. The winters up here are long and dreary. I hate the idea of them thinking it's all been a waste of time.'

'Oh, very well. I'll have a go. When?'

'I thought maybe this evening about seven-thirty at the village hall? I'll call for you.'

'You are persistent, aren't you? All right. I'll do my best.'

* * *

48

Before Hamish went out that evening to collect Mary, he turned on the six o'clock news. They had given quite a large coverage to the humiliation of John by the villagers. He felt suddenly uncomfortable. Surely John deserved it all, but the anger and violence of the villagers, highlighted by the camera, made him uneasy.

When Hamish drove Mary to the village hall, she kept nervously protesting that she did not have the talents of an editor. But once she got started, Hamish thought she did marvellously. She even got one of the locals to read out a translation of Alistair's work. She made tactful suggestions to each, but always throwing in a bit of praise, which made each villager glow with pride.

The evening was just winding up with the villagers crowding around Mary to thank her when the door of the village hall burst open. A crofter from Cnothan, Perry Sutherland, stood there, his face as white as paper.

'Hamish Macbeth!' he shouted.

'I'm here. What's the matter, Perry?'

'It iss thon writer. He hass killed himself.'

Hamish asked Angela to run Mary back to the hotel, then he sprinted to the police station, got in the Land Rover, and turned on the siren. He raced out of Lochdubh and on to the Cnothan Road.

The stars were bright and the night had

49

turned bitterly cold. The track to John's croft house was already hard under his wheels and frost shone like marcasite on the heather on either side of the track. Behind him in his car came Perry Sutherland.

The door of John's cottage was standing open with light streaming out. Perry joined Hamish. 'Was the door like that before?' asked Hamish.

'Aye, that's why I went in. I chapped first, and when I didnae hear nothing, I went in and found him on the floor.'

Hamish hurried into the cottage. In the living room John Heppel was lying on the floor. Hamish knelt down beside him and felt for a pulse. There was no sign of life. He sighed and sat back on his heels and looked around the room. The remains of an evening meal lay on the table. The room was icy cold. The computer was still switched on, and he could see something on the screen. He got up and went over to the computer. There was a message which read, 'I can't go on living any more. The people of Lochdubh have killed me.'

Hamish took out his mobile and phoned Strathbane police headquarters and reported the death.

Then he went back and stared down at the body. Surely no one as vain as John would take his own life. But if he had, how had he killed himself?

He pulled on gloves. He longed to search the

house but knew he would get a rocket from the forensic boys for leaving his footprints all over the place. He decided to have a look inside the dead man's mouth to see if that would give him a clue. He went back out to where Perry was shivering under the stars.

'They're on their way, Perry,' said Hamish. 'There's nothing you can do. Get into your car and switch on the heater.'

'This is a bad business,' said Perry. 'I saw him on the news. Do you think that's what did it?'

'I hope not,' said Hamish, thinking that if John had really committed suicide, he might become some sort of literary martyr crucified by wicked villagers.

Hamish searched for the kit he always carried with him in the Land Rover and drew out a tongue depressor. He went back in and knelt down again and felt the body. Rigor had not yet set in. He might have died recently. But Hamish knew that rapid cooling of a body could delay rigor.

He gently slid the tongue depressor between John's dead lips and opened the mouth a little. He could see that the tongue was black. He withdrew the depressor and looked around again. There was something nagging at the back of his mind. He got up and went to the fire. He noticed the peat was gleaming damply. He leaned into the fireplace and touched it. Then he stood up and frowned. He could swear water had been thrown on that fire to put it out.

Hamish could hear sirens in the distance. He removed his gloves, slid the tongue depressor into his pocket, and walked outside. The great oak tree growing over the cottage groaned in a rising north wind, and as one old branch rubbed against another, making a creaking sound, Hamish shivered and thought that a gibbet with a body on it would have sounded like that in the old days.

He hoped Detective Chief Inspector Blair was drunk or on leave or anywhere that would stop him from coming. His thick-headed, bullying ways had impeded many of Hamish's investigations. But his heart sank as the first police car arrived and Blair's heavy body heaved itself out of the back seat.

'Whit do we have?' he demanded in his heavy, truculent Glasgow accent.

'John Heppel is dead. He's left an apparent suicide note, but I think –'

'What you think, laddie, doesnae matter. We'll wait for the pathologist. She's on her way.'

'She?'

'Aye, they would go and appoint some damn woman. That's the trouble these days. They want to look all modern, so they shove some lassie into a job that should ha' gone to a man.'

'Who is she?'

'Professor Jane Forsyth. Here she comes.'

A little Ford drew up, and a stocky middle-aged woman got out. 'Where's the body?' she asked.

'It's in the living room,' said Hamish.

Hamish made to follow her, but Blair growled, 'Stay where you are.'

So Hamish stayed and looked up at the stars and shivered in the wind and wondered what it was that was nagging somewhere at the back of his brain. And suddenly he had it. John had signed the book for him with an old-fashioned fountain pen, the kind you refilled from a bottle of ink. There had been a bottle of ink on his desk.

He was sure that someone had either poured ink into John's mouth or made him drink it. That smacked of revenge. That smacked of murder. But he had somehow to get to the pathologist without Blair listening.

Detective Jimmy Anderson arrived. Hamish went to meet him. 'Jimmy, don't ask at the moment. Just get Blair out of there so I can have a sneaky word with the pathologist.'

'Cost you a bottle o' whisky. I'll need to lie. I'll need to say that Superintendent Daviot is particularly interested and wants him to phone right away.'

'What happens to you when Daviot says he doesn't know what Blair's talking about?'

'Daviot's attending the Freemasons tonight. Let's hope by the time he hears about this, he's really interested.'

Jimmy went into the house. I hope Blair doesn't take out his mobile or use John's phone, thought Hamish, but a minute later Blair shot out and went to the police car.

Hamish slid into the house and approached the pathologist. 'There are two things you ought to know,' he said, bending over her as she worked on the body. 'His tongue is black and I think it's ink.'

'Ink!' She stared up at him in surprise. 'What makes you say that?'

'I put a tongue depressor in his mouth to see if I could find out if he had taken anything. His tongue was black. He used an old-fashioned fountain pen.' Hamish looked across at the desk. 'There's an empty bottle of ink there. It was full the other night. Also, water's been thrown on the fire to put it out and delay rigor. Someone was trying to cover up the time of death. Don't tell Blair I looked in his mouth.'

They heard Blair lumbering back towards the cottage. Professor Forsyth quickly opened John's mouth just as Blair came in.

'How are you getting on, lassie?' said Blair.

'My name is Professor Forsyth, and I hope you will remember that in future. This man's tongue is black. Your intelligent officer here has just pointed out it looks like ink, and the ink bottle on the desk is empty. The fire has been put out, as if someone wanted to delay the onset of rigor. It could well be murder.'

'I told you to wait outside,' yelled Blair.

'Just as well he didn't,' said the pathologist.

'What about the suicide note?' demanded Blair.

'Anyone could have written that. I'll need to get this body removed to the lab for a proper autopsy. I shall send a report of my findings to the procurator fiscal.'

'If there are no prints on that ink bottle,' said Hamish, 'or on the keyboard of the computer, then that will definitely be suspicious.'

'Just get the hell out of here!' roared Blair. 'Go and look at your sheep or whatever it is you usually do.'

The professor gave a click of annoyance.

Hamish retreated. He decided to go back to the police station. Jimmy, lured by whisky, would visit him as soon as he could. As he left, he noticed the forensic team had arrived and were putting on their blue suits with tight-fitting hoods and bags drawn tightly over their shoes so that no trace of their own DNA should mess up a possible murder scene.

In the police station Hamish made himself a cup of coffee after giving Lugs a bowl of water and sat down to think before he typed up his report. It looked to him as if someone, some-how, had murdered John, maybe forcing him to drink the ink first. Then the murderer may have panicked and tried to fake a suicide, possibly wiping John's dead face to remove any external traces of ink.

Who had reason to hate John so much? There were the village members of the writing class. He had humiliated all of them.

'I hope it's not one of them,' said Hamish to Lugs. 'I knew that man would bring evil here.'

He sighed and went through to his computer in the police office, typed his report, and sent it off to headquarters. He had just finished when Jimmy Anderson called from the kitchen door, 'Anyone at home?'

'Aye, come ben,' shouted Hamish.

He closed down the computer and said over his shoulder to Jimmy, 'This is a bad business. How did it go after I left?'

'Give me a dram and I'll tell you.'

They went into the kitchen, where Hamish got down the whisky bottle and two glasses.

'I'll pour my own,' said Jimmy, seizing the bottle. They both sat down at the kitchen table.

'It's cold in here,' complained Jimmy.

Hamish rose and went to the stove. He raked down the ashes, put in kindling and threw a lighted match in. When it was all burning, he added several slices of peat and replaced the lid of the stove. He sat down again.

He looked steadily at Jimmy.

'Well, was it murder?'

Chapter Four

Like the dew on the mountain,
Like the foam on the river,
Like the bubble on the fountain,
Thou art gone, and for ever!
— Sir Walter Scott

'Thon professor seemed to think so. Blair is raging. He's due to go on holiday the next week, and he thinks you invented clues pointing to murder to spite him. Anyway, it looks as if the focus is going to be on that writing class here. Blair's coming over tomorrow to interview everyone.'

'I'd like to be there when he interviews the Currie sisters,' said Hamish. 'But you know Blair. I suppose I'm off the case.'

'Not quite. You're to make door-to-door inquiries.'

'Press arrived yet?'

'The Tommel Castle Hotel is beginning to fill up. They're a funny lot. What beats me is that by tomorrow there'll be some fellow standing

57

in front of the camera saying, "And here I am in the picturesque village of Lochdubh." Will anyone see a bit of the village? Not on your life. All they'll see is his big ba' heid in front of the camera.'

'Jessma Gardener is pretty good.'

'Fancy her, do you? What about that reporter lassie you were romancing?'

'She got a job in Glasgow.'

'Going down to see her?'

'Maybe.' Hamish realized with a little jolt that he missed Elspeth Grant. At first he had been relieved when she left. But all the good and bad times they had shared together came flooding into his mind and he wondered why he had ever let her go. Had she still been in Lochdubh, she would be sitting across from him with her frizzy hair and charity shop clothes, her silver eyes fixed steadily on his as she brought her uncanny psychic abilities to bear on the case.

'You should ha' married her,' said Jimmy, helping himself to more whisky.

'You're not a good advertisement for marriage,' said Hamish huffily. 'How many times? Three?'

'Two. Anyway, back to the murder. If it turns out to be ink in his mouth, then it looks as if someone offed him with hate and then tried to make it look like suicide. Everyone saw the hatred of the villagers on the telly. What about that brute Alistair Taggart? He's been done once for assaulting a fellow worker.'

'If John Heppel upset everyone here so much, then he must have upset a lot of people in his past.'

'Yes, but he wasn't murdered in Glasgow, he was murdered here.'

'He also did some work for Strathbane Television. Some sort of script. He told me he had done a script for *Down in the Glen*.'

'Have you seen that programme? It's a lowland Scots idea of the Highlands. All the women walk around in tartan shawls and the crofters in kilts. I mean, it's hardly high literature.'

'I think anything to do with television drew that man like a magnet. I'd like to take a trip over there, but no doubt Blair will be on the scene tomorrow to make sure I'm doing nothing other than chapping at doors and interviewing all the people who weren't at the writing class. I'd really like to know exactly how he was killed. But the autopsy will take a couple of days, and then the report will go to the procurator fiscal. Let me know as soon as you hear.'

'Keep the whisky coming and I'll let you know anything.'

Two days later Superintendent Peter Daviot received a visit from Professor Jane Forsythe.

'This is a most unusual murder,' she began. 'Have you got the report from the procurator fiscal?'

'Yes, but I haven't read it yet.' And in answer to her raised eyebrows, he said defensively, 'I've had a lot of work this morning.'

'I would like to go over to Lochdubh to discuss the case with that policeman.'

'Detective Chief Inspector Blair?'

'No, not that oaf. The tall one with the red hair.'

'That'll be Hamish Macbeth. Why him?'

'Because he has a shrewd intelligence. Besides, I don't like Blair's patronizing attitude.'

'He is a good detective.'

'Nonetheless, I would like to speak to that policeman. What's his name again?'

'Hamish Macbeth.'

Hamish had crept into his police station over the back field for a cup of tea. Somewhere out on the waterfront, Blair was pompously addressing the press.

The kettle had just boiled when there came a knock at the front door. Hamish assumed it was some reporter or other because all the locals knew to use the kitchen door. But his highland curiosity drove him to tiptoe to the front door and peer through the spyhole. He recognized Professor Forsyth. He shouted through the letter box. 'Could you come to the side door? This one sticks with the damp.'

He went through and opened the kitchen door.

'I have your superior's permission to call on you,' said the professor.

'Mr Blair?'

'No, not him. Mr Daviot.'

'Please come in,' said Hamish. 'I am just making some tea. Would you like a cup?'

'Please.'

'Sit down. Milk and sugar?'

'Both.'

Hamish searched desperately for a milk jug and then just put the bottle on the table. Then he fished in his trouser pocket and found some little packets of sugar he had taken from a restaurant table.

When he had poured her a cup of tea, he asked eagerly, 'How did he die?'

'Mothballs.'

'*Mothballs!*'

'Yes, naphthalene poisoning.'

'But he wouldn't have sat there and crunched mothballs.'

'Exactly. He had a weak heart.'

'Wait a bit. Surely a poison like that would induce vomiting?'

'It did. Someone cleaned him up and scrubbed the floor. It's a stone-flagged floor, but we found some traces between the stones.'

'There were rugs on the floor when I was there.'

'Indeed. Our killer must have taken them away.'

'And the ink?'

'The only way I can think to explain it is this: Perhaps the mothballs were melted by heat into black liquid. The liquid was mixed with whisky. Say someone held a gun on him and forced him to drink the mixture. When he started to vomit, his attacker watched him until he died and then poured ink into the mouth. Rage over, the killer suddenly decided to fake a suicide and closed the mouth and wiped off the excess ink. Then he scrubbed away the vomit and took away the rugs after typing that suicide note on the computer.

'I got John Heppel's medical records. He suffered from high blood pressure and his heart was weak. I should think he died very quickly. There would not be much vomit. I decided to call on you because it is the most interesting case I have come across. So hate-filled and elaborate. I saw the villagers attacking him on television.'

'It can't be one of them,' protested Hamish.

'Why not?'

'I can just about imagine one of them lashing out, but this one was planned.'

'Do you know anyone in Lochdubh who would have mothballs?'

'About everyone, I should think. I've got

them myself. I found my uniform had moth holes in it a while back, so I bought some mothballs from Patel's grocery.'

'But surely it must be someone in the village. This tea is very good, by the way.'

'It's the water. What about Strathbane? Heppel was doing something for television there. I'd like a word with them, but I fear Mr Blair would not permit it.'

'Give me a minute,' she said. Professor Forsyth took out her mobile phone and walked outside the police station.

After a few minutes she came back. 'I've just had a word with Mr Daviot. He says he will get Jimmy Anderson to meet you there.' She grinned. 'Mr Blair is to continue to interview the villagers. Any more of that tea?'

The Currie sisters, Nessie and Jessie, were ushered into the mobile police unit parked on the waterfront. Blair was sitting behind a desk, having finished with his press interview.

He eyed them with disfavour, thinking they would both look well in a production of *Arsenic and Old Lace*. They were identical twins with tightly permed white hair and thick glasses. Both wore long tweed coats smelling of mothballs.

'Sit down, ladies,' barked Blair.

They sat down primly on two hard chairs and faced him.

A rising gale outside shrieked around the mobile police station.

'I hope you've got this van well anchored down, anchored down,' said Jessie. 'The wind's awfy strong, awfy strong.'

'Forget about the wind,' barked Blair. 'Why did you murder John Heppel?'

'We didn't, you silly man,' said Nessie.

'Where were you on the Monday night when John Heppel was murdered?'

'At what time would that be?'

'Between five in the evening and ten.'

'That's easy,' said Nessie smugly. A great buffet of wind rocked the mobile police station, and the sisters held on to the edge of the desk.

'I said that's easy,' shouted Nessie above the shriek and roar of the wind. 'As representatives of the Lochdubh Mothers' Union, we were visiting the Strathbane Mothers' Union. We took the bus to Strathbane at four-thirty, and we didn't get back until after ten.'

'I'll check your alibi,' said Blair.

Both sisters rose to their feet.

'Oh, you do that, you daft auld man, auld man,' said Jessie.

'I'll hae the pair of you for insulting a police officer.' Blair got up as well.

At that moment there was a tremendous howling, shrieking sound approaching down the loch.

The sisters, who knew the terrors of the sudden Sutherland storms which sometimes came roaring in from the Atlantic, scampered for the door and flung it open and escaped on to the waterfront.

A few moments after they had left, a mini-tornado picked up the mobile police van and threw it like a child's toy into the loch before roaring on up and dying on the mountains.

Alistair Taggart, who had been sheltering in a doorway, ran across the road and down the steps to the pebbly beach. He stripped off down to his underpants, waded into the loch and began to swim.

Blair was struggling and gasping. 'I cannae swim,' he choked out.

Alistair grabbed him as he was about to sink. 'Lie still,' he shouted, 'and I'll pull you in.'

Two constables who had been with Blair were already battling for the shore. The press had erupted out of the local bar and were busy filming as the wind howled and roared.

Blair was carried by the villagers into the pub.

Jessma Gardener, soaked and shivering, held out a microphone to Alistair, who was being wrapped in blankets. 'You're a hero. What is your name?'

'Alistair Taggart.'

'What do you do, Alistair?'

Alistair looked straight into the camera lens. 'I am an author,' he said. 'I write in the Gaelic.'

Hamish found Jimmy in high good humour when he arrived at police headquarters in Strathbane. 'Hamish, you've got to look at this video I made of the lunchtime news.'

'I'm anxious to get started.'

'You cannae miss seeing this.' Jimmy slotted in a video. 'Sit yourself down, laddie, and be prepared for the show of the century.'

The windswept waterfront with the police mobile unit appeared. 'This is an amateur video from Mr Patel,' said Jimmy. 'The press were all in the pub at the beginning of the action.'

Hamish saw the mobile police unit begin to rock dangerously. The door opened and the Currie sisters hurtled out. The wind propelled them at great speed along the waterfront. Then there was an almighty roar, and the camera swung to catch a black funnel racing down the loch. Hamish watched, fascinated, as the mobile unit was lifted up like a toy and thrown into the loch. Then he recognized Alistair Taggart running across the road.

The camera work became more expert as the Strathbane cameraman took over. Jimmy and Hamish watched as Blair was rescued. Then the scene switched to the pub, and there was Alistair Taggart. 'His obsession for his writing must have taken over from his obsession with the booze,' commented Hamish. Alistair's normally drink-swollen face was lean and craggy. Alistair made his statement about being a writer and then shrugged off praise from Jessma on his bravery. Then the camera swung to show a shot of a wet and miserable Blair wrapped in blankets.

Jimmy switched off the video. 'It's a pity the auld bastard didn't drown. Let's go.'

Down in Edinburgh, literary agent Blythe Summer was giving last-minute instructions to his secretary. 'You hold the fort while I'm away. If I can sign up this Gaelic writer, I think we might make a killing.'

His secretary, Maggie Gillespie, looked doubtful. 'Who on earth can read Gaelic today?'

'Oh, it's become a sort of cult. There are classes all over the place now. There's a hotel up there. Book me in.'

Hamish had been at Strathbane Television before during a murder investigation. As he and Jimmy walked through the doors, he felt as he had felt before: that they were entering some sort of closed world. He knew the executive staff had all been changed since the last takeover.

At the desk they asked to speak to Harry Tarrant, the drama executive, and were told to take a seat and wait.

'The higher up they are,' said Hamish gloomily, 'the longer you have to wait. Have you seen *Down in the Glen*, Jimmy? Oh, I forgot. They usually only show sports in pubs.'

'I don't spend my life in pubs,' said Jimmy. 'Man, I thought you'd be in a better humour after seeing that video.'

Hamish shrugged. 'I don't know what it is about this place, but it gives me the creeps. Maybe it's because there are so many egos bottled up in the same building.'

'Come on, you crabbit copper. I thought that Jessma Gardener was pretty nice.'

'Maybe.'

A secretary approached them and said in accents of stultifying gentility, 'Mr Terrent will see you now.'

'I thought his name was Tarrant,' said Hamish maliciously.

She did not deign to reply but led them through double glass doors to a lift, ushered them in and pressed the button for the fifth floor. On the fifth floor they followed her through a long corridor to a door at the end. She knocked. A voice said, 'Come!'

I hate people who say 'Come,' thought Hamish.

She opened the door. 'The pelice er heah, Mr Terrent.'

A small man with a large black beard stood up from behind a massive desk. 'That will be all, Miss Patty. Oh, wait a minute. I am sure the gentlemen would like some coffee.'

'Please,' said Jimmy.

'Good, good. Sit down. Two coffees, Miss Patty.'

'What ever happened to women's lib?' asked Hamish when Miss Patty had retreated. 'I thought it was no longer politically correct to order secretaries to fetch coffee.'

'Bugger political correctness,' said Harry. 'That's all old hat. Women have finally woken up to the fact that they are subservient. Now, how can I help you? Is it about poor John?'

'It appears he was murdered,' said Jimmy. 'We wondered if he had bad relations with anyone here.'

'You surprise me,' said Harry. 'We are one big happy family here. How can you even think such a thing? You saw the hate in those villagers' faces.'

'Aye,' said Hamish. 'But you see, I know these villagers very well, and I cannot think one of them could commit such an elaborate murder.'

'You keep calling it murder,' said Harry. 'Last heard, poor John had left a suicide note.'

'We believe he was murdered with naphthalene,' said Hamish.

'What's that?'

'You get it from mothballs.'

'Then it must have been someone in Lochdubh. The whole place is mothballed. I went there once and I thought, set your watch back one hundred years.'

The door opened and Miss Patty came in carrying a tray with coffee jug, milk and sugar, and cups.

'Anyway,' went on Harry, 'I simply cannot believe that anyone would want to murder John Heppel.'

Miss Patty dropped the tray with a crash. Milk and coffee spilled over the carpet.

'You stupid girl,' roared Harry. 'Clean that mess up and get out of here! No, on second thought, leave it until the police have left.'

'I'm so sorry,' wailed Miss Patty.

'Sod off,' said Harry brutally.

He turned to Jimmy and Hamish. 'Where was I? Ah, yes, John. He was working on a script for us for *Down in the Glen*. Magnificent stuff. He was working on a second draft because the director wanted a few changes.'

'Who is the director?' asked Hamish.

'An English chap called Paul Gibson.'

'May we speak to him?'

'Not today. He's up round John O'Groat's way. On location.'

'When will he be back?'

'Tomorrow.'

Hamish produced a card. 'Would you please ask him to phone me? And I would like to see the script.'

Harry buzzed his secretary. When she appeared, Hamish noticed she had been crying. 'Get me John Heppel's script for *Down in the Glen*,' ordered Harry.

'Mr Gibson has it with him.'

'What's he doing carrying it around?'

'I don't know, I'm sure.'

'Okay, get lost. I'll call you.'

Miss Patty went out.

'Was it a good script?' asked Hamish while Jimmy threw him a bored look, wondering at all the questions.

'As I said, it was magnificent. I tell you, he had the right idea. Just because it's a soap doesn't mean that we can't have a literary script.'

'And what was the plot?' asked Hamish.

For the first time, Harry looked uncomfortable. 'Well, it was about a murder.'

'Describe it.'

'There's this brilliant writer, and all the other writers are jealous of him and he begins to receive death threats. He moves to the Highlands and falls in love with Annie, one of our main characters, who is being raped by the laird. It looks like suicide because the gun is found in his hand.'

'How original,' said Hamish dryly. 'I'll bet someone noticed he was left-handed but the gun was in his right hand.'

'How did you guess?'

'Just intuition,' said Hamish sarcastically.

'Anyway, the writing was pure Dostoyevsky.'

'You mean the man who wrote *The Idiot*?'

'Amazing. A learned policeman.'

Hamish had actually only read the title in the local mobile library when he was searching for a detective story.

'And you can't think of anyone here who might hate him?'

'No one at all.'

'Did you commission him to write a script, or did he approach you?'

'I had known him before.' Harry looked uneasy. 'We were friends in our youth in Glasgow.'

'In the slums?'

'Well, now, John was indulging in a little bit of exaggeration there. He was actually brought up in Bearsden.'

'That's pretty posh.'

'You see, working class is all the thing these days. If a writer comes from a cosy background and starts writing a book set in the slums, people might think he didn't know what he was writing about.'

'Did he always write?'

'He always tried.'

'What was he doing when you knew him?'

'He was an income tax inspector.'

'That's enough to get anyone murdered,' said Jimmy.

'My friend is dead,' said Harry coldly. 'I don't like your tone.'

'Who was he in contact with here apart from you?' asked Hamish.

'He had consultations with the director and the script editor.'

'And who is the script editor?'

'Sally Quinn.'

'May we speak to her?'

'I'll get Miss Patty to take you to her. Now I have work to do.' He buzzed for his secretary.

As Miss Patty led them to a staircase leading to the floor below, Hamish studied her with new interest. She was a small faded woman, possibly in her late thirties, with dull sandy hair and a pinched white face. Hamish felt suddenly sorry for her. She should have been secretary to a bank manager or had some sort of job away from this brutal world where she might get a bit of respect. Yet some people would put up with a lot to think they were part of show business.

'In here,' said Miss Patty, pushing open a door. 'Selly, pelice to see you.'

Sally was a tall, angular woman with frizzy grey hair and pale eyes behind thick glasses. 'I wish that silly cow would stop calling me Selly,' she said. 'It's the old Kelvinside accent. You hardly hear it these days. You've come about John's death?'

'Did you think his script had merit?' asked Hamish.

'Brilliant stuff. Never seen anything like it,' said Sally to the window.

'Did everyone here like him?'

'Of course. Sweet man,' Sally told the coffee pot on her desk.

'Why isn't there a copy of the script here?'

'Paul Gibson took all the copies with him on location. It wasn't quite finished, and so he thought he'd go over it while he was away. He'll be back tomorrow.'

Jimmy's phone rang. He took it out and moved to a corner of the room. Hamish heard his exclamation of surprise and then 'Right, sir.'

Jimmy rang off and turned to Hamish. 'Developments. We've got to go.'

They thanked Sally and walked outside.

'What?' asked Hamish.

'Blair has arrested Alistair Taggart for the murder.'

74

Chapter Five

Here lies one who meant well, tried a little, failed much: – surely that may be his epitaph, of which he need not be ashamed.
                    – Robert Louis Stevenson

The message they received when they arrived back at police headquarters was that Jimmy was to go immediately upstairs to join Blair and that Hamish Macbeth was to get back to his beat.

Hamish drove straight to Lochdubh, parked the Land Rover, collected Lugs, and walked up to Alistair Taggart's cottage. He knocked on the door. Maisie Taggart answered. Her eyes were red with crying, and she hugged her thin figure.

'He didnae do it,' she said on a choked sob.

'Can I come in?'

She nodded and turned away. He followed her into their living room. A battered typewriter stood on a desk in the corner with a pile of typescript beside it. I wonder where folks get ribbons for those things today, thought Hamish, what with most people using computers.

He took off his cap and sat down. Lugs slumped in a corner and went to sleep.

'Why do they think he did it?' asked Hamish.

'Thon Perry Sutherland says he saw Alistair up at John's cottage the night he was killed.'

'And why didn't Perry say this before?'

'He said he didn't want Alistair to get into trouble. Then that nasty fat detective kept shouting at him and accusing Perry of the murder, and that's when Perry said he'd seen Alistair.'

'Did they search your house? Did they find anything incriminating?'

'They found a packet of mothballs.'

'I've got a packet of mothballs. I think everyone in Lochdubh has a packet of mothballs. Why did Alistair say he was visiting John?'

'He went to get the money back he'd paid for the writing class.'

'And did he?'

'Yes.'

'Was he drinking?'

'No, he's sworn off. He just writes and writes. Drives me mad. At least when he was on the drink, he would pass out sooner or later and give me a bit o' peace. Anyway, I've had enough of him. I'm off to my sister in Oban.'

'But if they haven't any hard evidence, it'll never get to court and he'll be released.'

'Well, I won't be here waiting for him – him and his writing.'

'Surely that's better than the drink.'

A mulish look settled on her weak face.

Hamish repressed a sigh. He'd seen cases like this so many times before. The woman prays and prays that her man will give up the bottle, and when he does, she leaves him and usually moves in after a while with another drunk. These women had the awful craving to be needed, even if it meant lying for the drunk and cleaning up after him.

'You'd better give me your address in Oban,' he said.

'Why? Alistair's got nothing to do with me any more.'

Hamish said patiently, 'The police will want to interview you further. Don't you have to make a statement?'

'I've already talked to that fat bully. I told him Alistair went out at five and came back at six.'

'Give me the address anyway.'

She told him her sister's address, and he wrote it carefully in his notebook.

'And what about your son, Dermott? Won't he be upset at being taken out of school?'

'No, he says he'll be glad to get away as well.'

* * *

Outside, Hamish said to Lugs, 'We're off to Cnothan. If Perry saw him, maybe someone else saw him and heard something.'

He drove off to Cnothan, and as he was driving through that dreary village, he saw one of those itinerate door-to-door salesmen who sell dusters and brushes and stuff for the kitchen. He stopped the Land Rover and got out.

The salesman, a shabby young man, was just leaving one of the houses. Hamish hailed him.

'I've got a licence,' said the man defiantly. 'I haven't done anything wrong.'

'I just want to know if you went to any of the outlying cottages on the day that man was murdered.'

'Aye, I even went to that fellow's cottage afore he was murdered.'

'What time of day would that be?'

'Early evening. Not sure of the time.'

'And you saw him?'

'Only for a wee bit. He was having a blazing row wi' a big fellow. The big fellow was shouting, "I want my money back." And then the man what's now dead said, "Oh, take it and get lost."'

'Now, listen carefully. Did you see the big man drive off?'

'Aye, he jumped into a battered wee car and roared away. I went up to the door, but afore I could open my mouth it was slammed in my face.'

'You've got to come with me to the police

station and make a statement. It is very important. Have you transport?'

'I've got my bike.'

'You heard all about the murder. Didn't you think to talk to the police?'

'Why? I didnae do it and the man was alive when I saw him.'

'Right. Follow me.'

'Can you be giving me a bed for the night?'

'I've got one cell with a bed in it. You can use that and then return to Cnothan in the morning.'

'I've had enough of this place. I've never met such a bunch o' sour-faced bastards in my life.'

'Let's go.'

In the police station at Lochdubh, Hamish typed while the salesman – who gave his name as Hugh Ryan – talked.

'What did the man arguing with John Heppel look like?'

'He was thickset with grey curly hair and a sort of beat-up face."

'And what was he wearing?'

'A donkey jacket and jeans.'

'And the car?'

'A dirty white one with rust on the driver's side. I could see that from the lights shining out of the house.'

Hamish typed busily and then sent his report over to Strathbane. He grinned as he pressed the key to send it on its way, feeling as if he were launching an Exocet in the direction of Detective Chief Inspector Blair.

Blair was furious because Alistair Taggart had asked for a lawyer as soon as he arrived at police headquarters and there was the usual long wait until one could be found.

Jimmy Anderson was handed Hamish's report by one of the policewomen. He read it and began to laugh.

'What's so funny, Anderson?' demanded a voice behind him.

Jimmy twisted round and saw Superintendent Daviot standing behind him.

Jimmy stood up. 'I have just received this report from Hamish Macbeth, sir. It exonerates Alistair Taggart.'

'And you think that's funny? Give me the report.'

Daviot read it quickly and then snapped, 'Get Mr Blair out of that interview room and give him this.'

'Yes, sir.'

Blair was just getting into his bullying stride, ignoring the frequent interruptions of the lawyer, when Jimmy opened the door.

'A word with you, sir.'

Blair suspended the tape recorder and marched out. 'This had better be important.'

Jimmy handed him Hamish's report.

Blair read it once and then read it again, his face growing darker with fury.

'Mr Daviot has read it,' said Jimmy.

'Get over there and check out this salesman,' shouted Blair. 'I don't trust Macbeth.'

'I'd better take Mr Taggart with me,' said Jimmy. 'You'll have to release him now.'

How Blair longed to say he was keeping Taggart locked up. But Daviot had seen the report, and Taggart had a lawyer who might sue him for wrongful arrest if he kept him any longer.

'What's the time?' asked Alistair outside police headquarters.

'It's eight o'clock,' said Jimmy.

'Aye, well, just you drop me off at Strathbane Television.'

'Why?'

'Mind yer own business.'

In the living room of the Lochdubh police station, salesman Hugh Ryan was slumped on the sofa, fast asleep.

Hamish switched on the television to watch the nine o'clock news. The newscaster read out the international news and then said in a portentous voice, 'Tonight we have a special interview with Mr Alistair Taggart, who has just been released from police custody after

81

being falsely accused of the murder of John Heppel. Jessma Gardener has this exclusive report.'

First there was a rehash of the murder, including film of the violent villagers of Lochdubh shouting at John. Then the camera moved to the studio, where Jessma was facing Alistair.

'They've cleaned him up!' exclaimed Hamish.

Alistair's shaggy locks had been trimmed, and the costume department had kitted him out in a tweed jacket, corduroy trousers, and a roll-necked sweater.

'Now, Mr Taggart,' began Jessma, 'you have had quite a gruelling ordeal. Tell us what happened.'

Alistair had a pleasant voice with a highland lilt. Hamish waited for him to rant and rave, but Alistair said in a calm voice, 'I was working on my manuscript when Detective Chief Inspector Blair arrived at my cottage. He accused me of murder. Police searched the house and said they had found incriminating evidence.'

'And what was that evidence?'

'A bag of mothballs.'

'And that was all? I mean, a lot of houses have bags of mothballs.'

'Blair said it was because I had been having a row with John Heppel on the night he died.'

'And had you?'

'Yes, I went to get my money back for that writing class. I told him he was a fraud. I had a terrible time at the hands of the police. I am a writer, and we writers are sensitive.'

'Dear God,' muttered Hamish.

Someone handed Jessma a slip of paper. She read it and smiled. 'We have just learned that the reason for your release is because your local constable, Hamish Macbeth, diligently discovered evidence to clear you, which his superior officers had overlooked.'

'Hamish Macbeth is a very clever man,' said Alistair. 'It was because of him that I started writing. He inspired me.'

Jimmy Anderson had stopped in a pub on the outskirts of Strathbane before going on to Lochdubh. He tucked his mobile phone away and raised his glass to the television set at the end of the bar that was broadcasting the news.

'Credit where credit's due,' he said. 'And won't Blair just hate it!'

'Where did Strathbane Television get that bit about me?' demanded Hamish when Jimmy strolled into the police station.

'A little bird must have told them.'

Hamish eyed him cynically. 'I suppose the little bird wants a dram.'

'Aye, that would be grand. I've been sent to interrogate your witness all over again. But why bother?'

Literary agent Blythe Summer was up in his room at the Tommel Castle Hotel packing his suitcase. He had heard of Alistair's arrest and considered his journey wasted. A muted television set was flickering in the corner of the room, and as he folded shirts, he thought he heard the name Taggart. He turned up the sound and listened with rapt attention. Then he picked up the phone and dialled reception. 'I'll be staying for a bit, after all,' he said.

The next morning Alistair read over and over again the note his wife had left him. It simply said, 'I've taken Dermott to my sister's. Don't try to reach me. I don't want to see you again. Maisie.'

All his dreams of becoming a great writer fled. While he had been on television, he had imagined Maisie and his son watching him proudly. The fact that his drunken behaviour might have driven her away did not cross his mind. All he felt was black self-pity. He decided to go to Patel's and buy a bottle of whisky.

He put on the tweed jacket which he had

84

'forgotten' to return to the television costume department, opened his front door and found himself facing a round, dapper man carrying a briefcase.

'What?' demanded Alistair.

'I am Blythe Summer, literary agent, and I am interested in taking you on as a client. May I come in?'

Missing Maisie and thoughts of whisky fled from Alistair's head. 'Come ben,' he said. 'It's a bit of a mess.' Blythe followed him in and looked around for some uncluttered place to sit down.

'Did you see me on the telly last night?' asked Alistair eagerly.

'I did that. Writers who can get publicity for themselves are invaluable.'

'That's what I thought,' said Alistair proudly. 'When I left those bastards at police headquarters, I thought, I'm going to get something out of this.'

'May I sit down?'

'Just move those newspapers from the sofa. I haven't anything to offer you to drink.'

'It's too early,' said Blythe. He thought quickly. He had lost a few promising Scottish authors to the bottle. 'You know, the writers who succeed don't drink at all.'

'Is that a fact!'

'Absolutely.' Blythe opened his briefcase. 'Now to discuss terms.'

* * *

After saying goodbye to Hugh Ryan, Hamish felt he should go back to Cnothan to see if anyone else had seen someone visiting John on the fateful evening. But when he thought of Strathbane Television, he remembered there was something in the atmosphere there that nagged at him. He would travel to Strathbane, he decided, and see if he could speak to the director, Paul Gibson.

On the way to Strathbane he paid a visit to Dimity Dan's. The pub had the sour, hungover air of a place which had not been properly cleaned from the night before. A few tables still had dirty glasses on them.

He looked around but could see no one among the few customers who looked under-age.

Hamish decided to call again in the evening. Maybe Dan would let his guard slip, thinking that Hamish would not make another call that day.

Angela Brodie was looking after Lugs. Hamish found he missed his dog's company. I'll end up a weird old bachelor if I go on missing my dog, he thought. Elspeth hadn't written or phoned. Perhaps he might get permission to go to Glasgow and check on John Heppel's background and maybe see her. Then he struck his forehead. Of course! As a journalist, Elspeth would already have ferreted into the Glasgow end.

He pulled into a lay-by on a crest of the road overlooking Strathbane.

Hamish phoned the newspaper offices in Glasgow, asked for the reporters desk, and then asked for Elspeth. She came on the phone, sounding slightly breathless.

'It's me – Hamish. Elspeth, I'm working on this John Heppel case and wondered if you had any background on the man.'

There was a silence, and then Elspeth said in a cold voice, 'What ever happened to "How are you, darling? How's the job? Are you well?"'

'I wrote,' said Hamish defiantly.

'I suppose you did. I wasn't working on the John Heppel thing. Another reporter was. The background was in the paper. Didn't you read it?'

'I haven't had time,' said Hamish defensively. 'Wait a minute.'

Hamish held on, staring down at Strathbane, which lay sprawled under low-flying clouds, one great cancer on the beauty of the surrounding Highlands.

Elspeth came back on the line. 'I'll give you the main details. John Heppel was not brought up in a slum but in a tidy bungalow in Bearsden. He was an income tax inspector but was out of work for a while. He went into politics.'

'What politics?.'

'Some bunch of Trotskyites. Hurled a brick at a policeman during a demonstration and was jailed for three months due to the fact that his ailing parents got him a good lawyer and he had a clean record up till then. Parents now dead. No romantic involvement we could find.'

'What about friends? Was there by any chance a Harry Tarrant mentioned anywhere?'

'Now, that rings a bell. Wait a minute. The reporter who covered the story has just walked in.'

Hamish waited patiently.

After what seemed a very long time, Elspeth came back on the line. 'In the old report on that demonstration there was a Harry Tarrant arrested as well.'

'Great!'

'Why? Who's Harry Tarrant?'

'He's the drama executive of Strathbane Television, and John was writing a script for them. Are you enjoying yourself down there, Elspeth?'

'I don't know. I'm just another reporter here. I miss the independence I had up there.'

'You could always come back.'

'I'll think about it. I have to go.'

The news editor loomed over Elspeth after she had put the phone down. 'Not taking personal calls, I hope?'

'No, it was business. An old friend of mine, Hamish Macbeth, the local copper in Lochdubh, is working on that writer murder.'

'Might be an idea to send you up there. Now that most of the press will have gone, you might get a good story since you know this policeman and know the area.'

'Here!' complained Matthew Campbell, the reporter who had already been working on the story. 'Are you taking it away from me?'

'No, the pair of you can go. But go easy on expenses.'

Hamish drove on to Strathbane Television. He wondered whether to interview Harry Tarrant but decided to leave it for the moment. He asked for Paul Gibson.

A man not a lot older than Hamish finally appeared. He had thick curly grey hair and a mobile comedian's face.

'Am I under arrest?' he joked.

'No, just a few questions.'

'Let's go round the corner to the pub. I've had enough of this place for one morning.'

They walked round to one of those awful Scottish pubs which had just been redecorated with tartan carpet, bad murals of Highlanders brandishing claymores in front of a Bonny Prince Charlie with an epicene face. Syrupy piped Muzak sounded through the smoke-laden air.

Paul ordered a Malibu and milk. Hamish was always amazed at the new exotic tastes of drinkers. He ordered a mineral water for himself and carried both glasses back to a round table and sat down in a plastic chair with arms made out of simulated stag's horns.

'I want you to tell me all about John Heppel,' said Hamish.

'There's not much to tell,' said Paul. 'I wanted several changes in the script and told the script editor, and she got on to him.'

'But you must have met him?'

'Yes, he came with us on location to get a feel for the series.'

'And how did that go?'

'We had quite a pleasant time.'

Hamish leaned back in his chair and studied Paul's face. 'You must be the only person who ever had a pleasant time with John Heppel. You mean he just observed without interfering?'

'That's it.'

'I will be talking to members of the cast of *Down in the Glen*. I hope they will all back up your story.'

Paul gave a rueful shrug. 'You know how it is in show business.'

'No, I don't. Explain.'

'We get into the habit of never criticizing anyone. Oh, well, you'll probably find out. John was a major pain in the arse. He kept interrupting and criticizing the acting and criticizing the actors. I complained I couldn't work with him around, but Tarrant said I had to give him the best treatment. I need the work so I put up with it. I've directed soaps before and believe me, there's always someone who's a pill.'

'Did you ever go to John's cottage?'

'No. I don't even know where he lived.'

'Was he in any sort of romantic relationship with anyone?'

'Apart from spending his time halfway up Tarrant's bum, no, not that I know of.'

'Thanks for your time, Mr Gibson. I may get back to you.'

Paul opted to stay in the pub, and Hamish returned to Strathbane Television. He was about to ask for Harry Tarrant when his phone rang. It was Angela. 'Hamish, there's a whisper round the village that Callum McSween, the dustman, drove off after John – you know, after everyone had been shouting at him on the waterfront – and cut in front of his car, got out, and threatened him with a tyre lever.'

'Do the police know this?'

'No. You know what we're like here. We always try to protect each other, particularly from someone like Blair.'

'I'd better get back.'

Chapter Six

Murder most foul, as in the best it is;
But this most foul, strange, and unnatural.
                    – William Shakespeare

When Hamish returned to Lochdubh, villagers were still clearing up after the storm. Garden fencing was down, and tiles had been ripped off roofs. He had driven straight past Dimity Dan's but vowed to return on the following evening. He went up to Callum McSween's cottage.

The dustman was sawing branches off a fallen tree in his garden. 'Want a cup of tea, Hamish?' he called cheerfully. 'Thon was a right bad storm.'

'No, I need to talk to you, Callum. It's important. Do you mind if we go inside?'

The cheerfulness had left Callum's face. He walked into his small one-storeyed croft house. Hamish followed him into the kitchen. 'You've heard,' said Callum bleakly.

'Seems to be round the village. You followed John and threatened him with a tyre lever.'

'I wouldnae have hurt him,' pleaded Callum. 'You know me, Hamish. I wouldnae hurt a soul.'

'What exactly happened?'

'I was that mad at him because of the way he sneered at all of us, and him an incomer, too. I followed him in my truck, and at that one wide bit outside the Tommel Castle, I cut him off and made him stop. I told him he had to give us all our money back. I waved the tyre lever at him to frighten him. He got a big fright and he said he would. That's it. I moved my truck and he drove off.'

'Callum, if Blair gets to hear of this . . . well, you know what he's like. With that man, it's arrest first and ask questions afterwards. I'll not be saying anything about this for the moment. But I warn you, if Blair does get to hear of it, then you'll be in for a rough time. If that happens, just sit there and refuse to speak until they get you a lawyer.'

'Thanks, Hamish. I owe you.'

'In that case, keep your ear to the ground when you're on your rounds. You know what we're like up here. We can know something about someone, but if we think it'll get them into trouble, we don't say anything. Wait a bit. Do you pick up the rubbish from Dimity Dan's?'

'Aye.'

'I'm just wondering if you ever saw anything like a syringe or anything suspicious.'

'No. It may be a dirty pub, but he's right neat with the rubbish. Has it sealed up in wine boxes and things like that.'

'Does he now? Well, next collection day, do something for me. Keep aside some of those sealed boxes and take them round to the police station. I'll get you to sign a statement saying where they came from. When's the next collection?'

'Tomorrow.'

'At what time?'

'Six in the morning. Then I go to a good few of the outlying houses. I could be at the police station around ten.'

'I'll be waiting for you, unless Blair turns up and orders me somewhere else. If I'm not at the police station, take them home and phone me later.'

'Anything I can do for you, I will,' said Callum fervently.

When Hamish returned to the police station, he found the schoolteacher, Freda, waiting for him.

'Anything the matter?' asked Hamish.

'No, it's just that you said you might like to go clubbing. I'm off to Inverness this Saturday. Would you like to come?'

'Let's see what happens,' said Hamish. 'I'm in the middle of this murder inquiry. You don't happen to have heard anything that might help?'

'No, not a thing,' said Freda to the table. She's lying, thought Hamish. I wonder why.

But instead he asked, 'When would you be leaving for Inverness?'

'Round about eight o'clock. Do you mind driving if you decide to go? I like a drink or two.'

'No, I don't mind. But I'll drive your car. If Blair sees me with a civilian in the police car, he'll blow his top. Leave your phone number with me. Would it be all right if I decided to go with you at the last minute?'

'That would be fine.' Freda took out a notebook and wrote down her mobile phone number.

At the newspaper office in Glasgow, Elspeth Grant was complaining to Matthew Campbell about their delayed departure for the north. Another story involving the talents of both of them had cropped up, and they estimated it would be Saturday morning before they could get off.

'Was this copper a boyfriend of yours?' asked Matthew.

'No,' lied Elspeth. 'Just a friend.'

* * *

Hamish was curious about Miss Patty, Harry Tarrant's secretary. Maybe she was just over-sensitive. But her reaction to the news of John's murder seemed extreme. He longed to get back to Strathbane, but Blair wanted all the villagers who had been at the writing class interviewed again and had given Hamish a list of those he most suspected. At the top were the Currie sisters.

Hamish knew that this probably simply meant they had got Blair's back up, but duty was duty. And the only thing that kept the maverick Hamish in line was the fear of losing his precious police station in Lochdubh.

He hoped that the sisters might have taken themselves off somewhere, but Nessie answered the door to him with a sharp 'What now?'

'Mr Blair wishes me to ask you some more questions.'

'Come ben. I suppose you'll want tea.'

'No, thank you.'

'Nonsense, you always want tea. Aren't we always saying in the village that Hamish Macbeth wouldn't pay for a cup of tea if he could get one free? Sit down!'

'I don't want tea,' snarled Hamish, but Nessie was already in the kitchen, and he could hear her talking to her sister.

'Put the kettle on, Jessie. Thon Hamish Macbeth is here, looking for free cups of tea as usual. His superior has told him to ask us

97

some more questions, and does Macbeth stand up to him? No. Spineless.'

'Spineless,' echoed her sister.

Hamish sat with his face flaming red with irritation.

The sisters eventually bustled in with a loaded tray. 'Here's your tea,' said Jessie, 'your tea.'

Hamish placed his cup on one of those pieces of furniture called an occasional table, and took out his notebook.

'Our alibi checked out,' said Nessie before he could open his mouth, 'so there is no use you wasting your time going over that again.'

'I was going to ask you if either of you or both of you called on John Heppel before you went to Strathbane.'

Hamish had simply asked that question out of irritation. He did not think for a minute they had, but Jessie's teacup rattled in its saucer and she shot a quick glance at her sister, who said, 'We were in Strathbane and you are wasting time.'

'Wasting time,' murmured Jessie.

Hamish studied the two faces. Their eyes behind their thick glasses were blank.

'Wind's back again,' said Nessie as the window panes rattled.

'You were at John's cottage,' said Hamish. 'You see, I know you were.'

'She said she wouldnae say anything,' cried Nessie.

Another thought leapt into Hamish's mind. He remembered he had thought Freda was holding back something, and he had assumed that something was Callum's visit.

'Freda, the schoolteacher,' said Hamish. 'You'd better tell me about your visit.'

'It was nothing,' said Nessie. 'We wanted our money back, so we drove up to his cottage.'

'Why didn't you drive to Strathbane?' asked Hamish, momentarily diverted.

'It's too far. It's better to take the bus. So we saw that John Heppel, and he was very rude. He said he had given us his valuable time and he wasn't giving any money back. Then young Angus said . . .'

She put her hand over her mouth.

'Out with it!' ordered Hamish. 'Just how many of you went up there? I'll find out, you know.'

'It was at four in the afternoon. Oh, you may as well know. There was us and Angus Petrie, Mrs Wellington and Archie Maclean.'

'Dear God, ladies. Do you know the trouble you'll all be in when Blair gets to hear of this?'

'Have a scone, a scone,' said Jessie eagerly.

Irritated, Hamish was about to shout that he did not want a scone, but the one held out to him on a plate looked feathery light and was laden with butter and what appeared to be home-made strawberry jam.

He took the plate.

'You see,' said Nessie eagerly, 'that bullying fat man need never know. None of us would tell him.'

'I can't be keeping information like that out of my report!'

They watched him as he bit into the scone.

'You wouldn't have known if thon Freda had kept her mouth shut,' said Nessie.

Hamish finished the scone. 'She didn't say anything,' he confessed. 'It was just a lucky guess.'

'So there you are!' exclaimed Nessie triumphantly. 'We were all up there long afore he was killed. Have another scone.'

Hamish left a quarter of an hour later, full of scones and guilt. He had made a rash promise to keep quiet about their visit unless Blair or any policeman found out. Then he would need to put in a report, and fast.

He made his way up to the manse. Mrs Wellington answered the door and said quickly, 'I'm too busy.'

'Why didn't you tell me you'd seen John Heppel the day he was murdered?'

Mrs Wellington flushed red. 'You'd better come in.'

Hamish followed her into the large manse kitchen, a relic of the days when ministers had large families. A huge scarred wooden dresser took up one wall, and along another wall was the old coal-fired range, never used now for cooking but only for heating the room. A gas cooker was against the third wall beside two enormous porcelain sinks.

Hamish wondered suddenly if the Wellingtons minded being childless. But then, he reflected, he could never imagine the Wellingtons doing what was necessary to make a child. He could not imagine Mrs Wellington out of her tweeds. He sometimes wondered madly if she wore a tweed nightgown.

'Sit down,' she barked militantly as if trying to regain her dignity.

Hamish took off his cap and sat down at the kitchen table.

'I didn't report it,' she said, 'or Mr Blair would have arrested me. I mean, look what happened to Alistair Taggart.'

'I sympathize with you,' said Hamish. 'I don't think I can keep it quiet very long. You should know that these things come out sooner or later. He wouldn't have arrested all of you. You were all there before Heppel was murdered, so what was the harm in telling the police? Oh, well, the damage is done. Now, I want you to think hard. I know you were all very angry. But imagine you're back there. He wouldn't let you in his house. Do you think there was anyone else in there?'

Mrs Wellington sat very still. 'There might have been. He stood with the door just open a little so we couldn't see past him.'

101

'And how was he? Could he have been frightened?'

'Hard to tell. He was flustered and angry. He shouted a lot of nonsense that he was a celebrity who had given us his valuable time. Angus Petrie made a dash for the door and he slammed it shut. Archie Maclean kicked the door and shouted. Then we went away.'

'What did Archie shout?'

Her head went down and she avoided his eyes. 'I can't remember.'

'I'll be asking Archie myself. Now, as you walked away, were you aware of any other vehicle there?'

She shook her head.

'Did you pass anyone on the road?'

'Not on the road to his house, not on the track. No one for a bit and then a grey van.'

'What make?'

'I think it was one of those little old Ford vans.'

'Light grey? Dark grey?'

'Sort of light grey and dirty.'

'Any markings? Anything written on the side?'

'No. But I wasn't paying any particular attention.'

'You wouldn't happen to have remembered any number plate? Even a letter?'

'No, I'm sorry.'

'And where exactly did you pass this van?'

'Just before we got to Cnothan.'

'They were all in your car?'

'Yes.'

'I'd better go and see Angus Petrie and see what he has to say. If you remember anything else, phone me.'

Hamish collected Lugs and drove over to the forest on the other side of the loch. He went to the forestry office and asked for Angus.

'He's up the hill a bit,' said the manager. 'You can take that Land Rover of yours straight up the track. I hope the lad's not in any trouble. He's a good worker.'

'Just routine inquiries.'

Hamish went out and got into the Land Rover and drove up a broad track between the pine trees, which were beginning to bend in the rising wind.

At the top of the track he stopped where a group of men were sitting drinking tea, Angus amongst them.

Hamish climbed down from the Land Rover and went round to the passenger side and lifted Lugs down. The dog ran off through the trees.

'Angus Petrie,' said Hamish. 'A word with you.'

Angus reluctantly left the group and walked over to the Land Rover.

'Now, Angus, I know you were up at John

Heppel's cottage the afternoon before he was murdered.'

'Who telt ye?'

'It doesn't matter now. I've spoken to the Currie sisters and Mrs Wellington.'

'But I didnae kill him!'

'I'm not saying you did. I'm going to have a hard job keeping this away from Blair, and the only reason I'm doing it is because he'd be crashing around and arresting you all and the whole investigation would slow up. What I'm really interested in is your impressions. You may have seen or heard something you might have forgotten. When John answered the door to you, did you get the feeling that there might be someone inside the cottage?'

'I never really thought. I was that angry. He stood with the door a wee bit open.'

'And you weren't aware of anyone outside apart from yourselves?'

'No.'

'Now, on the road back before you got to Cnothan, you passed a van.'

'I didnae notice anything on the road. I was still mad, you see. But I tell you this, Hamish Macbeth, I'm going to go on writing. Thon nice lady writer thought I should.'

'I don't know how long I can keep your visit quiet, Angus, but I want you to think hard. Like I said, there may be something important you've forgotten.'

* * *

Hamish drove back to the police station. He fed Lugs and then set out for Strathbane. He was anxious to talk to Miss Patty again.

As he left Lochdubh, he saw the door-to-door salesman, Hugh Ryan, leaving the Currie sisters' cottage. He stopped and called to him. Ryan walked over. 'They're polite here,' he said. 'I'll give you that. But I cannae even sell a duster.'

'I'm off to Strathbane. Why don't you try some of the housing estates there?'

'Maybe.'

'Or try the Tommel Castle Hotel. Tell the manager I sent you. They always need more cleaning stuff.'

Hamish drove off. A rising wind had moved round to the north-east, and little pellets of snow were beginning to dance crazily in the air.

Hamish swore under his breath. No snow had been forecast, and the gritters hadn't been out to lay salt. He hoped they'd get to it soon, or he would have an evening of being called out to road accidents.

But as he drove down into Strathbane, the snow changed to sleet and then rain. A wet mist was beginning to blanket the town, a mist made hellish orange by the sodium light of the street lamps.

He parked at Strathbane Television and asked at the desk to speak to Miss Patty.

While he waited, he tried to sort out in his head the complexities of the case. It couldn't have been anyone in Lochdubh, could it? But Highlanders are ultra-sensitive creatures, and John had wounded so many egos. It had been a hate crime.

Miss Patty appeared, flustered and nervous.

'I would like to talk to you,' said Hamish. 'Is there anywhere we can go that's private?'

She hesitated and then said, 'Mr Terrent is out this efternoon. There is a keffy next door. Perheps . . .'

'Yes, that'll do. Do you want to get your coat?'

'No, it's right next door.'

To Hamish's relief, the café was run by Italians, which meant hot coffee and clean tables. He bought them both coffee and then they sat down.

'Miss Patty,' he began, 'I noticed you were extremely upset at the news of the murder of John Heppel.'

'Yes,' she whispered.

'Was he more to you than just a scriptwriter?'

She flushed an ugly red. 'No.'

'Are you from Strathbane?'

'No.' Her thin ringless hands wrapped themselves round the coffee cup for comfort.

'Where are you from?'

'Glasgow.'

'Glasgow! Which part?'

The genteel accents suddenly left her, and she demanded harshly, 'Why? What's it got to do with you where I come from?'

'I thought you might have known Mr Heppel years ago.'

'No.'

'If you are lying, Miss Patty, I can find out. What is your first name?'

'Alice.'

'Right, Alice. When did you get the job up here?'

'Two years ago.'

'That would be after the last takeover. Was the job advertised in the Glasgow papers?'

'Yes.'

Hamish leaned back in his chair and surveyed her. Never lie to a Highlander, lassie, he thought cynically. We've all got master's degrees in bullshit.

'I think you knew Harry Tarrant in Glasgow. I also think you knew John Heppel. I think you met them when you were a member of the Trotskyites.'

'I have nothing more to say to you.' She banged down her cup and jumped to her feet. 'I've got to get back.'

'Sit down,' barked Hamish, 'or I'll have you for obstructing a police investigation.'

She sat down again. All traces of refinement had gone. Her face had hardened, and her mouth was set in a stubborn line. 'Give me your home address,' he ordered.

'I don't see —'

'Address! Now!'

'Ten Swan Avenue. I'm off, and next time you want to talk to me, pig, you can do it through my lawyer.'

She stormed out, and this time Hamish let her go.

He went back to his vehicle and took out a map of Strathbane and looked up Swan Avenue. It was in one of the better residential districts, out towards the Lochdubh Road.

He drove out there and turned on to Swan Avenue and found number 10. It was a trim little villa. He noticed there were two bells. She must rent either the upstairs or the downstairs.

He went to the door and pressed both bells. A small elderly man answered. 'What's happened?' he asked, staring at the uniformed policeman.

'Does Miss Patty live here?'

'Yes, she rents upstairs, but she's at work at the moment.'

'May I come in? I would like to ask you a few questions.'

'Yes, come in. The place is a bit of a mess. I live here alone and I never was one for housekeeping.'

The living room he led Hamish into was impeccable. Hamish wondered what his idea of a mess was.

'Your name, sir?' said Hamish, taking off his cap and laying it on one of those knee-high tables which must be the cause of more bad backs than anything else, people having to stoop every time they reached for a cup of something.

'Barry Fraser. What's all this about Miss Patty?'

'I'm investigating a murder. Miss Patty is not a suspect. We merely like to get background on everyone. Does she have any men friends?'

'Not lately.'

'But she did have?'

'There was this one chap who came a couple of times. Wee man with a black beard.'

Harry Tarrant, thought Hamish.

'Anyone else?'

'I don't know. She had a hell of a row with some fellow about two months ago. At first I didn't think it was her because she normally speaks in that prissy voice of hers. She was shouting, "You used me, you bastard. I'll tell Harry." Then the man shouted back, "He won't do anything. You're a rotten lay."

'"I'll kill you," she shouts, and then she throws a vase at him as he was leaving by the front door.

'When I went out, the man had gone, she was sitting at the top of the stairs crying, and there were bits of a glass vase in the hall where it had crashed against the door. I gave her a warning. I told her to clean up the mess and if she ever created a scene like that again, I'd tell her to leave. Nothing bad happened after that, and she pays her rent regularly.'

'Thank you,' said Hamish. 'I'd be grateful if you didn't mention my visit to her.'

'I hope she's not in any trouble. I mean, apart from that one incident, she's been an ideal tenant.'

'I'm sure you've got nothing to worry about.'

Hamish left and climbed into the Land Rover. He could not put in a report about Miss Patty because Blair would start howling about him being on Strathbane turf.

He phoned Jimmy Anderson and told him all he had found out. 'Great stuff, Hamish,' said Jimmy. 'Do you think the man she was shouting at could have been John Heppel?'

'Could have been. Don't tell Blair I've been in Strathbane.'

'Don't worry. I'll take all the credit for this. I'll get her in for questioning. I'd better go and see this neighbour myself and start from there.'

Chapter Seven

But to us, probability is the very guide of life.
— Bishop Joseph Butler

Hamish had a leisurely breakfast the following morning, and then he took Lugs for a walk. He could not see any police about the village, and he was puzzled by their absence. Surely Blair had not decided to leave a murder investigation to the local copper.

At ten o'clock, just after he had returned to the police station, Callum, the dustman, knocked at the door and presented Hamish with one of the sealed boxes of rubbish he had collected that morning from Dimity Dan's.

'Come through to the office,' said Hamish. 'I'll type up a statement for you to sign, saying that you thought the method of rubbish disposal suspicious and decided to take one of the boxes to the police station. I'd like another witness when I open the box.'

There was another knock at the door. When Hamish answered it, he saw Freda there.

'Come in,' he said. 'I'm going to need another witness.'

'What for? I came to ask you if you were going to Inverness this evening.'

'Let's see how we get on with this. I think Dan Buffort at Dimity Dan's is dealing drugs. He aye wraps up his rubbish in sealed boxes. I've got Callum to bring me one, and I'd like you to witness the contents. Make yourself a coffee while I type out something for Callum to sign first.'

Freda put a kettle on the stove and looked around. The kitchen was warm and neat. While she waited for the kettle to boil, she wandered into the living room. It had a bleak, little-used air. She guessed that Hamish spent most of his time in the kitchen. While she busied herself making coffee, she wondered what it would be like to be a policeman's wife. The police station was built like a croft house – one-storeyed, whitewashed, and with a slate roof. Freda wondered why Hamish did not make use of the loft space. Most crofters made the bedrooms up there, leaving extra space downstairs.

She made herself a coffee, sat down at the kitchen table, and mentally redecorated the house. The kitchen for a start. That old-fashioned wood-burning stove was ridiculous. It wasn't as if it even had an oven. It surely had been there for over a hundred years. There was a gas cooker with four jets and an oven, but it looked as if it had been little used. She was just mentally hanging bright curtains at the kitchen windows when she heard Hamish call her.

'Now we open this box,' he said. He took out a penknife and slit the tape which sealed the box.

'Pooh!' said Freda as a rancid smell floated up from the box. Hamish spread newspapers on the floor and tipped out the contents of the box. Amongst the potato peelings, sandwich wrappers, old cooked vegetables, two dead mice and bits of meat he found several little empty cellophane packets. He picked one up and sniffed at it. There was a little powder in one. He stuck a gloved finger in, then raised it to his nose.

'That's heroin. What else do we have?'

Freda's stomach was heaving from the smell. She was beginning to think that the lot of being a policeman's wife might not be a happy one, after all.

'Aha!' said Hamish. He carefully took out a little pill packet. There was one pill left in it. 'Got him!' crowed Hamish. 'Ecstasy!'

He carefully put all the rubbish back in the box apart from the ecstasy packet and the cellophane packets.

Hamish sat down at his computer and began to type. 'You two can wait in the kitchen,' he said, much to Freda's relief.

When he had finished a statement to the effect that the opening of the box had been witnessed by Callum McSween and Freda Garrety, he called them in to sign it.

'Are we going to Inverness tonight?' asked Freda.

'Not now this has come up,' said Hamish. 'The place will need to be raided. Thanks, both of you.'

When they had left, he phoned Strathbane. He spoke to Jimmy, who said that Blair was questioning Alice Patty.

'Oh, Lord!' said Hamish. 'She'll clam up.' He told Jimmy about the evidence of drugs.

'Great,' said Jimmy. 'I'll get back to you and tell you when we're going to raid the place.'

Hamish waited and waited. At lunchtime he went out to the shed where the freezer was and fished out a packet of lamb chops, which he defrosted by soaking them in hot water. Then he fried them up and gave half to Lugs and ate the other half himself.

He washed the dishes and stared at Lugs, who grinned back – or who looked in his doggy way as if he were grinning.

'It iss no laughing matter,' said Hamish, the sibilance of his accent showing just how annoyed he was. 'They should haff called by now.'

He went through to the office and phoned Strathbane and demanded to speak to Jimmy.

He had to wait a long time, and then Jimmy's breathless voice came on the line.

'Sorry, Hamish. Blair's just coordinating a raid for tonight.'

'What time?'

'Ten o'clock. But Blair doesn't want you to be there.'

'What!'

'Daviot seemed to think it was Blair who had done the detective work, so he doesn't want you getting any credit. He's very excited and wants to go on the raid.'

'Daviot, you mean?'

'Aye, the big cheese himself.'

'Blair's a bastard.'

'Well, it's your own fault, Hamish. You could have been down here with us ages ago if you weren't so hell-bent on staying in the peasants' paradise.'

Hamish slammed down the phone and stared at it. Then he picked it up and dialled Freda's number. 'I'll be free to go to Inverness, after all.'

Elspeth Grant stole a sideways look at Matthew Campbell, who was driving. He wasn't bad-looking, she thought. He had a shock of sandy hair and a round, cheerful face. The only problem was he enjoyed the sort of reporting they had been doing and Elspeth was beginning to hate it.

The last story they had worked on together concerned the odd case of a Glasgow man charged with the rape and murder of a twelve-year-old girl, although no body had been found. Matthew and Elspeth had been told to work on the background before the case came up in the High Court. Their job was to keep the Crown witness, the accused man's wife, away from the other press and the police. The trouble was the wife, Betty McCann, worked in a brothel. Elspeth's first introduction to a Glasgow brothel was an unpleasant one. It was housed in an old Victorian tenement flat. Betty was thirty-five and looked fifty-five with her toothless mouth, raddled face, and two inches of black showing on her dyed-blonde hair.

Matthew and Elspeth had been instructed to keep her away from the other press by taking her out to a hotel on Loch Lomond. The hotel was rather grand, and the manager protested bitterly about the filth Betty had left in the bath and the head lice she had left on the bed.

Then on the day of the trial, as they arrived with Betty outside the High Court, a frustrated reporter from the opposition punched Elspeth in the face and Matthew leapt out and gave him the Glasgow kiss – butting him on the face with his forehead.

Then Betty in the witness box had taken against the judge and called him a deaf old bugger when he asked her to repeat an answer.

116

But surely, Elspeth had thought, it would all be worth it after Betty's husband had been found guilty, so they typed up all the background to the story and looked forward to seeing their bylines prominently displayed in the morning edition.

Not one word appeared. When they demanded the reason, they were told that the editor had decided their background story was too fish-and-chip – too sordid for a family paper – and had spiked the lot.

Elspeth had never thought she would long for the days when she wrote the astrology column for the *Highland Times* and covered everything from shinty matches to dried flower arrangement competitions. And her psychic abilities appeared to have deserted her in the city as if blocked out by all the sordidness.

'It's going to be late by the time we reach Inverness,' said Matthew. 'Let's book into a hotel and have a decent dinner and we'll go north first thing in the morning.'

'All right,' said Elspeth, thinking it would be nice to have a hot bath and a change of clothes and make-up before she saw Hamish Macbeth again.

As they crossed the highland line and the Grampian mountains reared up on either side of the car, Elspeth's pulse began to quicken. She was going home again.

* * *

Hamish eased back the driver's seat of Freda's little car to accommodate his long legs.

'You're wearing a suit!' exclaimed Freda. 'Never tell me you've got a suit on under that coat of yours.'

'It iss my best suit.'

'You don't go clubbing in a suit. You wear casuals. Jeans. Stuff like that.'

'I cannae be bothered going back to change,' said Hamish huffily. 'I'll take my tie and jacket off.'

Freda was beginning to regret having asked him. What would her friends make of him?

Elspeth and Matthew made good time and reached Inverness much earlier than they had expected to.

But the prospect of dinner beckoned, and so they decided to stick to the original plan of setting out for Lochdubh in the morning.

When dinner was over, Matthew said, 'It's early yet. What's Inverness got in the way of amusement?'

'There are a couple of clubs.'

'What about dropping into one for a drink? I'd like to see what the local talent looks like.'

'All right. But not for long. We can walk. It's round the corner from this hotel.'

'Good,' said Matthew cheerfully. 'Now I can have a really big drink.'

* * *

Hamish Macbeth was not enjoying himself. Although still in his early thirties, he felt old and crotchety. Where was the fun of being jammed on a small dance floor where the music hurt his ears and the air was thick with smoke, cheap perfume and sweat?

Freda had cast off her long winter coat to reveal that she was wearing nothing more than a cropped top and a tiny red leather skirt. Hamish had left his jacket in the cloakroom along with his tie. The dancing came as no problem to him: it seemed to consist of jumping around and waving his arms in the air.

I wish I hadn't brought him, thought Freda. Her friends, the ones she had made since first visiting the club, were sitting over in the small bar area staring at them.

When the dance number finished, she said, 'I would like a drink.'

'I've got to go to the men's room,' said Hamish. 'I'll join you in a minute.'

'What are you drinking?'

'Give me a minute and I'll get them when I come back.'

Freda's friends, Cheryl, Sharon and Mary, moved along the banquette they were sitting on to make room for her.

'Who's the boyfriend?' asked Cheryl.

'He isn't my boyfriend. He's the local bobby.'

'He's got gorgeous red hair,' sighed Sharon.

'I was dancing up next to him. I'd give any-thing for eyelashes like that.'

Freda looked round at them in amazement. 'You fancy him?'

'Who wouldn't?' sighed Mary.

At that moment Hamish appeared. 'What are you all having to drink?' he asked. They all ordered Bacardi Breezers. Gloomily Hamish went to the bar. It was going to be an expens-ive night. He ordered the drinks and then a tonic water for himself. 'Where are the glasses?' he asked the barman.

'They all drink from the bottle here,' said the barman.

Hamish made his way back to the table and sat in a chair facing Freda and the girls.

The disco music started again just as they were beginning to speak. Conversation was nearly impossible.

Elspeth came on to the dance floor, and as she gyrated with Matthew, she glanced across at the bar and stumbled. 'Sorry,' she shouted in Matthew's ear. 'I've just seen Hamish Macbeth.'

'The bobby?'

'That's the one. He's at the bar.'

'Let's join him.'

Hamish slowly rose to his feet as he saw Elspeth approaching. She looked more soph-isticated than the last time he had seen her.

Her thick hair had been defrizzed, and she was wearing it in a French plait. She was dressed in a tailored blouse and skirt and high heels. Gone were the charity shop clothes and clumpy boots.

'What are you doing here?' he shouted.

'On that murder story. Can we have a word with you outside?'

He nodded.

Freda got up and followed him. Her interest in Hamish was awakened anew by her friends' admiration of him. Besides, who was this woman?

Hamish turned round in the doorway and saw Freda following. 'This is business, Freda. If you like to wait inside, I'll come back for you.'

'And dance by myself? A date's a date, Hamish.'

'All right. We'd best get our coats. It's freezing outside and you haven't got much on.'

Matthew and Elspeth were already outside. 'Let's find a pub,' said Matthew. 'I was only in there a few minutes and I'm deaf already.'

'You haven't introduced us, Hamish,' said Elspeth, looking at Freda.

'Oh, sorry. Freda, this is Elspeth Grant, who used to work for the *Highland Times*. Elspeth, our new schoolteacher, Freda Garrety.'

'And I'm Matthew Campbell,' said Matthew. 'There's a pub on the other side of the street.'

'More noise, probably,' said Elspeth. 'Let's use the hotel bar.'

In the hotel, after they had sat down in the bar, Elspeth covertly studied Hamish. Did he remember making love to her? As if picking up her thought, Hamish blushed and stared at the table.

Freda's eyes darted suspiciously from one to the other.

The waiter came up and they all ordered drinks. Hamish stuck to tonic water, although he suddenly felt that a whisky would be nice. Then he thought a cigarette would be even better. He had given up smoking but was still occasionally haunted by a yearning for nicotine.

'Now, Hamish,' began Elspeth, 'we're going up to Lochdubh in the morning to do a background piece on this murder. Any other press around?'

'No, they've given up apart from checking every day with headquarters in Strathbane. There isn't much I can tell you aside from what's been in the papers.'

'Tell us from the beginning,' said Matthew. He looked curiously at Hamish. He sensed Elspeth's tension and had seen Hamish blush. Surely she hadn't. Had she? Some of the already rebuffed reporters were going around saying she was a lesbian. But then, they said that about every girl who turned them down.

Hamish began to talk about the writing class and the bruised egos of the would-be writers. He described the murder and the false arrest of Alistair Taggart.

'It's bound to be one of those people in the writing class,' said Matthew

'I don't think so,' said Hamish stiffly. 'I know them all.'

'I don't think you know the violence of the humiliated writing ego,' said Matthew. 'Elspeth, do you remember that new reporter who got struck with a fit of the Hemingways? He wrote this news story which went something like this: Constable Peter Hammond was patrolling his beat on a foggy night in the mean streets of Glasgow. The fog muffled noise apart from the shrill sound of a child crying. He remembered his youth . . . and on and on and on until in the last paragraph he gets to the point and says someone shot him.

'The news editor went ballistic and tore it up in front of him and told him to write a proper news story. The reporter screamed that he had written a literary work of art and tried to strangle the editor, and it took three of us to haul him off.'

'No one in the village,' said Hamish firmly.

'Then if not in the village, where?' asked Matthew.

Elspeth studied Hamish with those odd silver eyes of hers, Gypsy eyes. 'What about Strathbane Television?' she asked.

'Why there?' asked Hamish cautiously.

'He was writing a script for *Down in the Glen*. If he was as nasty as he appears to have been, he could have riled someone there. Wait a bit. You asked me about the Trotskyites. Harry Tarrant was there at the time. Has he got an alibi for the time of the murder?'

'I don't think anyone asked him,' said Hamish. 'It's Strathbane's job, but they always walk on eggshells when it comes to television.'

'We'll ask him,' said Matthew cheerfully.

'Let me know what he says.' Hamish turned to Freda. 'I've got to start work early tomorrow. Would you mind if we went home?'

Freda pouted. She had intended to dance until the small hours. But returning with Hamish meant she could get this policeman whom her friends found so attractive all to herself.

On the long road back to Lochdubh, Freda chattered about this and that, but Hamish replied in monosyllables. He was engulfed with an odd longing for Elspeth, and yet he had not thought about her all that much since she had left for Glasgow.

Was Matthew Campbell just another reporter? They seemed very much at ease in each other's company.

He got out of the car at Freda's home. She put her face up to be kissed, but he didn't notice, his thoughts being still focussed on Elspeth.

What a waste of an evening, thought Freda, watching his long figure make its way along the waterfront to the police station.

One of the many faults of Detective Chief Inspector Blair was that as soon as the press lost interest in a case, he was apt to lose interest in it as well. He had put the murder of John Heppel to the back of his mind and the investigation to the back of his workload. He was in a bad mood because although the raid on Dimity Dan's had been successful – drugs found along with teenage drinkers – his moment of glory had been all too brief.

Hamish Macbeth had sent over a computerized report on how he had asked Callum to deliver the box of rubbish to the police station; it contained a statement from Callum and witness statements from Freda and Callum as well. Somehow the report had found its way to his boss's desk. Daviot had sent for him the morning after the raid. Fortunately Blair remembered in the nick of time that it was Peter Daviot's daughter's birthday and rushed out and bought a huge box of chocolates and a card.

'That is so kind of you. Sheila will be delighted,' said Daviot, who adored his eldest daughter. 'I must say, you're quite like one of the family.'

And the blistering lecture he had meant to give Blair was modified to a mild reprimand. 'I'm surprised you did not mention Macbeth in your report.'

'I'm right sorry, sir,' grovelled Blair. 'It must ha' slipped my mind. I should ha' given Macbeth the credit. But I think there's a reason for that. Macbeth insists on being a village bobby, and somehow you don't think of the village bobby when it comes to a major raid.'

'You have a point there,' said Daviot with a sigh. 'How is the investigation into the murder of John Heppel going?'

'We're still working on it.' Blair was suddenly struck with what he thought of as a brilliant idea. 'I was thinking of pulling my men out of Lochdubh,' he said, omitting to say that he already had, 'and letting Hamish Macbeth get on with it. Softly, softly approach, sir. He knows the locals.'

'Are the press still interested?'

'No, they've given up.'

'Let's try Macbeth for, say, a week, and see how he gets on.'

The following day Matthew and Elspeth booked in at the Tommel Castle Hotel. Matthew had talked on the road up as the landscape grew wilder about how he loathed

126

the countryside and how he would always be a city boy at heart. But as he walked outside the hotel after a very good lunch, the day was crisp and clear and the sun was shining. He breathed in the pure air and stared up at the soaring mountains. He would never have believed that a part of the overcrowded British Isles could be so deserted.

Elspeth appeared behind him. 'Admiring the view?'

'It's pretty breathtaking.'

'Nowhere else like it. There are Atlantic seals in the harbour, golden eagles on the mountains, and red deer on the moorland. You can find places where you can walk miles and see nothing made by man.'

'You love it here, don't you?'

'Yes, but I'm ambitious, too. There's not much up here for the ambitious. We'd better get started. Strathbane Television first.'

'I must say the food at this hotel is cordon bleu standard.'

'That's Clarry, the chef. When Hamish was a sergeant, Clarry was his sidekick. But he spent all the time cooking until he discovered that was all he really wanted to do.'

'Why did Macbeth get demoted back to constable?'

'It's a long story. I'll tell you sometime.'

They got in Matthew's car and drove off. 'How come Sutherland is so empty?' asked Matthew.

'It's because of the old Duke of Sutherland. At the start of the nineteenth century he owned the biggest private estate in Europe. It amounted to some one and a half million acres and covered a huge part of northern Scotland. He discovered he could get more money from grazing sheep than from the crofters. This caused the brutal removal of up to fifteen thousand people from the Duke of Sutherland's estates to make way for the sheep. Some were resettled in coastal communities like Lochdubh to take advantage of the herring boom. More were shipped abroad: many to North America. The clearances fundamentally changed the landscape of much of northern Scotland. The tiny settlements were swept away, leaving the occasional ruins you can see dotted about. There's a row going on still about the duke's statue in Golspie.'

'What row?'

'There's a hundred-foot-high statue on the top of Beinn a' Bhragaidh. It was erected a year after his death by, to quote, "a mourning and grateful tenantry to a judicious kind and liberal landlord." An awful lot of people want it pulled down.'

'See their point. Do we go straight to Strathbane Television, or do we call at police headquarters first?'

'The television station, I think.'

'I've often wondered,' said Matthew, 'why you settled for working for the *Daily Bugle*'s

Scottish edition. You could have gone to London. I only heard the other day that the main office had made you an offer.'

'Oh, I don't know. Maybe I didn't want to be too far away from the Highlands.'

'Glasgow's far enough away for me. I've never been further north than Inverness. It's a whole different world up here. You know how it is these days. The Scots don't want to holiday in Scotland any more. They want the sun. It's cheaper to take a holiday in Spain than book into some of these hotels in Scotland.'

They drove on in silence as the road wound through rocky clefts where tumbling waterfalls cascaded down, across heathery moorland, the single-track road winding in front of them until they crested a hill and Matthew exclaimed, 'What's that doing there?'

'That is Strathbane. Our very own area of pollution.'

The town lay in a valley below them, dark and ugly. The sun was disappearing behind the clouds, and a last ray shone on the oily waters of the deserted docks.

'What do they do for a living?'

'Collect their dole money, spend it on drink or drugs, and then go out and mug people for more money. That's the tower block lot. There's a respectable section of the population: small factory owners, lawyers, dentists, doctors, shopkeepers, schoolteachers, people like that.'

'And television people?'

'Apart from the odd secretary or two, I don't think you'll find any local people. Make two right turns on Ferry Street and then a left.'

'Was there a ferry?'

'There was at one time. It went out to Standing Stones Island, that lump you can see away out on the water. No one lives there now. They say it's haunted.'

'That would be a good feature. A night on the haunted island.'

'You're on your own on that one.'

'I might give it a try,' said Matthew.

'Left!' ordered Elspeth. 'Here we are.'

Miss Patty was being interrogated at police headquarters, so it was a bouncing blonde with bouncing cleavage who escorted Elspeth and Matthew to Harry Tarrant's office.

Harry greeted them warily, told them to sit down, and asked them what they wanted.

'We gather that you knew John Heppel quite a time ago when you were both members of the Trotskyites,' said Matthew, plunging right in.

Harry stiffened and then gave a jolly laugh. 'Ah, the follies of youth.'

'Can you tell us what sort of person he was?' asked Elspeth.

'Fine man,' said Harry. 'A really good writer.'

'How did he come to be writing a script for you?' asked Matthew.

'He e-mailed me and said it was difficult to write in the city. I suggested he come up to the Highlands for a bit of peace and quiet. I asked him if he would like to try his hand at writing something for television.'

'Why *Down in the Glen*? Hardly demands a literary script,' Elspeth pointed out.

'That's where you're wrong,' said Harry. 'Soaps can be educational – should be educational. I thought we needed to go upmarket with some serious writing.'

'I'm sure the police have asked you this.' Elspeth studied Harry's eyes. 'Where were you on the evening John Heppel was murdered?'

'Minding my own business,' snapped Harry, 'and I suggest you do the same.'

Matthew took out his notebook and began to write. 'Harry Tarrant said yesterday that he refused to state where he was on the evening of the murder,' he said out loud.

'Wait a minute.' Again that forced jolly laugh. 'Scrub that out. I've nothing to hide. I went for a drive. It had been a tough day and I find driving soothes me.'

'Where did you go?'

'Ullapool. I dropped in at the Fisherman's Arms for a drink and then drove back. It's a long drive. I must have left around six o'clock and got back at eleven o'clock and went straight to bed.'

'Had John made any enemies in the television company?'

131

'No, everybody was very impressed by him. Now, if there's nothing more, I have work to do.' He buzzed for the secretary to show them out.

As they were walking along one of the long corridors, Elspeth said to the secretary, 'I forgot to ask Mr Tarrant for a publicity photograph for our files. Can you get me one?'

'Sure. Just wait in reception and I'll bring you one.'

'Now what?' said Matthew outside.

'Ullapool,' said Elspeth. 'It's about an hour's drive. We've got the photo of him. Let's ask in the Fisherman's Arms if he was there.'

'What's Ullapool like?'

'Very pretty. Lots of tourists in the summer. They like to take the ferries out to the Summer Isles, uninhabited isles, to look at the seabirds and dolphins. Won't be very busy now.'

As they drove off, Matthew grumbled, 'The sun's gone down already. Does it never stay light up here?'

'You don't know much about your own country,' said Elspeth. 'In high summer it's nearly light all night.'

Hamish was at that moment sitting in John Heppel's cottage. He knew the place had been fingerprinted and thoroughly searched. But contrary to what people saw on television about forensic detection, he knew the forensic team from Strathbane were sometimes sloppy, particularly if there was a football match on television.

It was then that he noticed the computer was still on John's desk. Why on earth had it not been taken away and a thorough search made of the contents?

He moved over to John's desk and switched on the computer and went to Word and clicked into the files. He stared in amazement. There was nothing there. No record of the suicide note.

He opened the desk drawers. The police had taken all the papers out of the desk, but why not check the computer? He tapped the e-mail icon. To his surprise John's password was logged in. He went to the Inbox. No messages at all. He was sure someone, probably the murderer, had wiped everything clean. But surely some computer expert down at Strathbane could check the hard drive.

He phoned Jimmy Anderson and was told he was out. He then dialled the pub next door to police headquarters. Jimmy came on the line. 'What's this, Hamish? Can't I have a quiet drink?'

Hamish told him about the empty computer. 'Someone's slipped up there,' said Jimmy. 'You'd better bring it over here.'

'How's Miss Patty getting on?'

'Blair's interviewing her, and I gather the lassie's getting hysterical.'

'Does that scunner never realize he could get more out o' people by being nice for a change?'

'Never has, never will. See you when you bring that computer over.'

Hamish switched off the computer. There was a split second during which his highland sixth sense was suddenly and violently aware of danger. Then a heavy blow struck him on the back of the head.

'I can see it might be pretty in the summer,' said Matthew as he drove down into Ullapool, 'but it looks wet and miserable today.'

The weather had performed one of its usual mercurial changes. Sheets of fine rain were driving in off a heaving sea in a rising gale.

They parked in the municipal car park and began to walk down to the waterfront. Elspeth clutched Matthew's arm. 'Something's wrong,' she said.

'What? Time of the month?'

Elspeth shook her head as if to clear it. 'I felt something bad,' she said uneasily.

'It's that rich lunch we had,' said Matthew. 'When my stomach's upset, it does funny things to my brain. Where's this Fisherman's Arms?'

'Not far.'

'I'm soaked. I can hardly see anything for the rain.'

'It's what we call a grand soft day,' said Elspeth. The wind whipped her umbrella out of her hand and sent it sailing into the harbour. 'Oh, let's run!'

They charged into the Fisherman's Arms and shrugged off their soaking coats.

'I want a double whisky before I ask anyone anything,' said Matthew.

'You're driving.'

'So what?'

'So go ahead and I'll drive back. I'll have a glass of white wine.'

Matthew returned with the drinks. 'Wait till I get this down me and then we'll both go to the bar and start asking questions.'

Elspeth tasted her glass of wine cautiously. She reflected she should have known better than to order white wine in a bar. It tasted like vinegar.

'Right,' said Matthew when he had gulped down his whisky. 'That's better.'

They walked up to the bar, where a diminutive highland barmaid was staring vaguely into space. Apart from Elspeth and Matthew, there were only two other customers.

Matthew handed over the photograph of Harry Tarrant.

'We're reporters from the *Daily Bugle*,' he said. 'We're reporting on that murder in

135

Cnothan. Did this man come here on the day of the murder?'

'When was that again?'

'The seventeenth.'

'Aye, so it was. I wisnae here. Big Jake was on duty. You'd best ask him.'

'Where do we find him?'

'Sullivan Road. The housing estate up the back o' the town. Number 5.'

'Is it far? Should I go back to the car park and get the car?' asked Matthew.

'No. It's just a toddle. Go to the end and turn left. You'll see the council houses up on the hill.'

The walk in the driving rain turned out to be a long one, and by the time they reached Big Jake's address, they were soaked to the skin.

A man in dirty pyjamas answered the door. He was tall with a long thin face. His grey hair was thinning on top, but he had a long ponytail at the back.

'Big Jake?' asked Matthew.

'Aye.'

'We're reporters from the *Daily Bugle*. Can we come in?'

'No. I'm busy.'

Matthew fished out the photograph of Harry. 'Can you tell us if this man was in the Fisherman's Arms the evening John Heppel was murdered over in Cnothan?'

'Aye, that's him. I mind him well. I said if he drank ony mair, I'd need to take his car keys off him.'

'He was there all evening?'

'About three hours.'

'Was he with anyone?'

'No, sat by hisself drinking whisky.'

'Jake!' called a woman's voice from inside the house.

'Like a told you,' said Jake, 'I'm busy.' And he slammed the door.

'What a wasted day,' grumbled Matthew as they bent their heads before the rising storm and hurried back to the car. 'I've an awful feeling in my bones we're no' going to find much to write about.'

But he was wrong.

Chapter Eight

When constabulary duty's to be done,
The policeman's lot is not a happy one.
                                    – W. S. Gilbert

After Matthew and Elspeth had arrived back at the Tommel Castle Hotel and had changed into dry clothes, they met in the bar.

'We'll need to find something to write,' said Elspeth.

'Couldn't we just stay in this nice hotel for the evening and start tomorrow?'

'No, I think ... Oh, good evening, Mr Johnson.'

'Shame about Hamish Macbeth,' said the manager.

Elspeth's eyes widened in shock. 'What's happened to Hamish?'

'He was up at John Heppel's cottage when someone struck him a sore blow on the head. Perry Sutherland saw the cottage door lying open and went in and found him.'

'Where is he?'

'Over at Braikie Hospital.'

'Come on, Matthew,' said Elspeth.

The waiting room of Braikie Hospital was full of villagers from Lochdubh. Mrs Wellington strode forward to meet them. 'They're only allowing us in two at a time,' she said. 'You'll need to wait.'

'How is he?' asked Elspeth.

'He had a bad blow to the head, but they say he is only slightly concussed. It's not serious.'

'Who's with him now?'

'Miss Garrety, the schoolteacher.'

'And who's with her?'

Mrs Wellington gave a sly smile. 'We all agreed to let her go in on her own. It's time Macbeth was married.'

'Is there a canteen in this place?' asked Matthew.

'Yes, on the first floor.'

'Come along, Elspeth. We'll get a cup of tea while we're waiting.'

When they were out of earshot, Matthew said, 'I've got a plan.'

'Like what?'

'Let's go down to the basement instead. Maybe there's a laundry room there where we could disguise ourselves and jump the queue.'

'We'd be spotted. We can't cover our faces.'

'We can if we find some surgeons' stuff.'

Fortunately the basement area appeared to be deserted. They tried door after door. Most were locked.

'Someone's coming,' hissed Elspeth.

'In here!' urged Matthew, reopening one of the doors he knew was unlocked.

They waited. There was a sound of squeaking wheels. Matthew opened the door a crack.

A hospital porter was trundling a laundry basket on wheels. He went into a door at the end of a long corridor. Matthew waited. The man reappeared and walked down past where they were hidden.

When he had gone, Matthew said, 'I know where the laundry is. Come on.'

They hurried along to the laundry room. 'The stuff'll be dirty,' complained Elspeth.

'Then we'll pick out the least dirty ones.'

Freda sat by Hamish's bed and held his hand. 'Are you sure you feel all right?'

'I'd feel better if someone from police headquarters would arrive and tell me why that computer was never checked.'

The door opened and two masked figures entered. One said to Freda, 'You'll need to leave, miss. We have to take Mr Macbeth to the operating theatre.'

'What's this?' cried Hamish in alarm. 'No one said anything to me about needing an operation.'

The smaller of the 'surgeons' held open the door and said pointedly to Freda, 'If you don't mind, miss.'

When Freda had gone, Elspeth jerked down her mask and said, 'Surprise!'

'What the hell are you two doing?' exclaimed Hamish. 'Trying to give me a heart attack?'

'We checked Harry Tarrant's alibi,' said Elspeth. 'It checks out. Tell us what happened to you.'

'I was looking at John Heppel's computer. It had been wiped clean, but I wondered why it had been left behind. Surely some computer expert could have recovered stuff from the hard drive. Then someone hit me on the head.'

'And the computer was gone?'

'That was the reason for hitting me on the head,' said Hamish impatiently.

The door opened and Jimmy Anderson walked in. Matthew and Elspeth jerked up their masks and walked out.

'Press?' asked Jimmy, staring after them.

'Yes.'

'Oldest trick in the book. You don't need surgery, and yet here are two masked surgeons in dirty robes in your room. I hope they catch something awful. Who were they?'

'Couple of reporters from the *Bugle*. One was Elspeth Grant.'

'Ah, your ex-squeeze.'

'Never mind her. Tell me, Jimmy, why that computer was left there.'

'Well, the cops are blaming the forensic team, and the forensic team are blaming the cops. I think it was because it was a black laptop on a black desk. They didn't notice it. Daviot is blaming Blair, and Blair is blaming everyone he can think of. They're getting on to the server to see if they can retrieve anything that might have been in the e-mails.'

Hamish leaned his bandaged head back on the pillows. 'You know the trouble? We're dealing here with a rank amateur who killed in a fit of spite and rage and then tried to cover it up. I wish the villagers had never attacked John Heppel and been filmed for television doing it. It's taken the whole focus away from Strathbane Television. At least the press have their uses. Harry Tarrant was nowhere near Cnothan on the night of the murder. Oh, the magic of television. No one asked him where he was on the night of the murder.'

'Don't be so high and mighty. We didn't ask him either.'

'I would like to see a copy of that script for *Down in the Glen*,' fretted Hamish.

'Why?'

'There might be something in there. I don't know.'

'When are they letting you out?'

'Tomorrow, I hope.'

'For the sake o' decency, you should stay in longer. There's half the village waiting to visit you and they're all carrying gifts.'

'No, the sooner I get out of here, the better. My dog! Who's looking after my dog?'

'Your dog's waiting like everyone else. Angela Brodie's looking after him.'

By the time the last of the villagers had gone, Hamish felt quite weak and weepy. Their kindness was overwhelming. The room was crowded with presents of cake, jam, flowers, chocolates, and even two trout.

He decided that the best thing he could do was to find out where they were filming the next episode of *Down in the Glen* and go along and study everyone there. I hope you're looking in the right direction, said his conscience. You're so anxious to prove that it wasn't one of the villagers that maybe you haven't investigated your home turf enough.

The phone beside Hamish's bed rang, jerking him out of his worried thoughts.

Jimmy Anderson's voice came on the line. 'Worse and worse, Hamish. Blair's been suspended, pending an inquiry.'

'But that's good news.'

'He's been suspended because Miss Alice Patty has committed suicide by slashing her wrists. She left a note blaming police brutality. Patty's lawyer said that by the time she got in to see her at police headquarters, Blair's bullying had reduced the girl to a nervous wreck.'

'So are you in charge?'

'No. They've brought in a detective chief inspector from Inverness, Heather Meikle.'

'What's she like?'

'I'll tell you tomorrow. She arrives tomorrow.'

The next day Freda drove to the hospital as soon as school classes were over. Hamish had phoned her and asked for a lift to the police station. He had said he was checking himself out of the hospital.

She wondered whether she should have done something like make him beef tea. Freda decided to urge him to go to bed and then she would minister to him. As she drove off, she noticed several Strathbane Television vans parked on the waterfront. She hoped nothing else horrible had happened.

When she arrived in Hamish's room at the hospital, it was to find him dressed and sitting waiting for her. His bandages had been removed, but part of his fiery-red hair had been shaved off and a sticking plaster put over the wound.

As she drove off with him in the direction of Lochdubh, Freda said, 'I think when we arrive, I should make you something to eat and then you should go straight to bed.'

145

'No, I'll be all right. I'm sick of bed. I've been in bed for most of the day.'

'I still think you should rest. There are a lot of television vans on the waterfront at Lochdubh.'

'Anything happened?'

'Not that I know of.'

'Any press there?'

'No.'

Hamish's interest quickened. 'Maybe they're using Lochdubh as a location for that soap. Where's Elspeth?'

'I don't know. Running around with that boyfriend of hers.'

'He's not her boyfriend. He's just a colleague.'

'That's not what I heard,' lied Freda.

'You shouldn't listen to village gossip. They always get it wrong.'

'Are you keen on Elspeth?'

'The only thing I am keen on is getting to the police station and finding out if police headquarters have any idea of who hit me,' said Hamish stiffly.

Freda began to wish she'd arranged some sort of welcome at the police station for him. All the villagers knew where the spare key was kept – in the gutter above the door. She could have placed a bowl of flowers on the kitchen table. She could have lit the stove.

When she drove up to the police station, she

noticed the lights were on. 'Someone's there,' she said. 'Should I call the police?'

'I am the police. It's probably one of the villagers.'

He opened the kitchen door and walked in. Elspeth was sitting at the kitchen table. There was a bowl of flowers on the table and the stove was blazing away.

'I phoned the hospital and heard you were on your way,' said Elspeth. 'There's a casserole in the oven.'

Hamish turned to Freda, who was glaring at Elspeth. 'Thanks very much for the lift, Freda.'

Although he was obviously waiting for her to go, Freda plumped herself down at the table opposite Elspeth and asked, 'Any chance of a dram?'

'You sit down, Hamish,' said Elspeth. 'I'll get it.'

Freda began to wish she had left. There was an atmosphere between Hamish and Elspeth – an atmosphere which seemed to exclude her.

There was a knock at the door. 'I'll get it,' said Freda. Matthew came in.

'Elspeth,' he said, 'they're going to be filming *Down in the Glen* here tomorrow. The director, Paul Gibson, is at the bar at the hotel. I thought we could see him together.'

'What about the producer?'

'There isn't one. Gibson's title is producer-director. It's a way of cutting costs, I suppose.'

'Right. I'll get my coat. I left it in the bedroom.'

'Thanks for everything, Elspeth,' said Hamish.

Freda brightened. With Elspeth gone, surely Hamish would invite her to have supper with him. But no sooner had Matthew and Elspeth left than there was another knock at the door.

'What now?' asked Hamish.

A severe-looking woman stood on the doorstep. 'Good evening, Constable.' she said. 'I am Detective Chief Inspector Meikle.'

'Come in,' said Hamish. 'Freda, do you mind? This is police business.'

Freda left in a bad temper. Perhaps if Hamish had shown any interest in her, she would not have bothered about him. But she regarded Elspeth as competition, and besides that, her friends had found Hamish attractive. Men are credited with having hunter instincts, but women have them as well, and all at once Freda was firmly determined to marry Hamish Macbeth.

Heather Meikle took off her coat and handed it to Hamish. He hung it on a peg by the door.

'How's your head?' she asked.

'Seems all right. What brings you?'

She sat down at the table in the seat vacated by Freda and clasped her hands in front of her.

Heather Meikle was a tall woman with a

148

sallow face and short brown hair. She had a long thin nose and a thin mouth. She was dressed in a tailored suit and sensible shoes.

Her eyes were of an indeterminate colour and were now fixed on Hamish Macbeth with a piercing stare. 'I discovered that a major murder inquiry had been turned over to a village policeman,' she said.

'I noticed there weren't any other police around,' said Hamish cautiously.

'I may say, I have never heard of anything more ridiculous in my life. Proper investigations will resume tomorrow. I saw the news film of the villagers shouting and throwing things at Heppel. Any one of them could have committed murder from the looks of them.'

Hamish again spoke cautiously. 'It is my opinion, ma'am, that not enough attention is being paid to the television people. John Heppel was an infuriating man. Very vain. He liked humiliating people. He was addicted to getting his face on television. They are filming *Down in the Glen* here tomorrow. It's a good opportunity to talk to the director and the cast.'

'I think you might be letting your loyalty to the villagers mislead you. I want you to concentrate on them.' Her stomach gave a rumble.

Hamish wanted rid of her but was trapped by the rules of highland hospitality.

'I have a casserole in the oven,' he said. 'Would you like some?'

She hesitated and then smiled. 'That's very kind of you. I didn't have time to eat.'

Hamish laid out knives and forks and plates and lifted the casserole out of the oven, where it had been kept warm on a low heat. 'This is a present,' he said, 'but it looks like venison.' He spooned out two generous helpings. He was glad Lugs was still with Angela. The dog would have created merry hell until he got some.

He uncorked a bottle of red wine and put two glasses on the table. 'What kind of wine is it?' Heather asked.

Hamish read the label. 'I got it from Patel's the other week. It just says red wine.'

'Oh, well, I'll try it. I'm staying at the Tommel Castle Hotel for the one night. My driver is up at the hotel. I sent him back and told him to wait for my phone call, so I can have a drink without breaking any laws.'

She ate with a hearty appetite and drank most of the wine. 'You have a reputation for resisting promotion,' she said. 'Why?'

'Local police stations are closing down all over,' said Hamish. He did not want to tell her that he had no ambition whatsoever. People never understood that. 'I feel I have a duty to the highland communities. Someone's got to keep an eye on the old people living up on the moors.'

'If you say so. I wish Blair hadn't literally bullied that secretary to death.'

'It definitely was suicide?'

'Oh, yes, she left a very clear suicide note, typed on her computer, blaming Blair.'

'It *was* a suicide note? I mean, it wasn't the draft of a letter she meant to send to the newspapers or police headquarters?'

'Yes, of course.'

'Can you tell me exactly what it said?'

'I've got a copy somewhere. Have you any coffee? And a brandy would go nicely with it.'

Hamish went through to the living room and rummaged in a cupboard by the fire. There was a bottle of brandy that someone had given him two Christmases ago. He was just straightening up from the cupboard when Heather appeared in the living room. 'It's more comfortable in here,' she said. 'Why don't you light the fire?'

'I haven't lit a fire in here in ages,' said Hamish. 'I think the chimney needs to be swept.'

'Oh, I'm sure it'll be all right. Light the fire and make the coffee, and then I'll show you the letter.'

I wonder if marriage would be like this, thought Hamish sulkily. But he retreated to the kitchen and put the kettle on to boil. Then he returned to the living room and put kindling and paper on the fire and, when it was burning, added slabs of peat.

When she was seated with a tumbler of brandy – she had poured it herself – she rummaged in her capacious handbag and produced a black notebook. 'Here we are. She said, "The bullying of that man Blair is more than I can stand. The police brutality has shocked me. I'm getting out of this. You should be sorry but you won't be sorry."'

'And that's it!' exclaimed Hamish. 'Did she sign it?'

'No, but she cut her wrists in the bath, and the note was left on the floor beside the bath.'

'Who did she mean by "you"?'

'The world in general, I suppose.'

'She had been having an affair with her boss, Harry Tarrant, and I think she might have been having an affair with John Heppel as well. What was the toxicology report?'

'I haven't had the autopsy report yet. Too soon. What are you getting at?'

'Our murderer tried to make John Heppel's death look like suicide in a clumsy and amateurish way. Maybe he's got a bit more expert. I mean, that could have been a draft of a letter. How was the paper? Had it been cut top or bottom?'

'Why?' Heather reached forward and picked up the brandy bottle and refilled her tumbler.

'Well, just suppose she's writing a letter on her computer and prints it off. Say someone drugs her and alters the letter so that all that appears is what you've got. No "Dear" anybody or address.'

'You're wandering in the realms of fantasy, Officer.'

'But was her computer checked? They forgot about John Heppel's computer.'

She went through to the kitchen. Hamish heard her talking rapidly on her mobile phone.

Heather came back. 'They say there's no sign of the note she typed, but why would she save it? Anyway, to humour you, I told them to get an expert to recover what he can from the hard drive.'

'And how long will that take, ma'am?'

'Forever and a day. It's being sent down to Glasgow. That fire looks as if it's going out.'

Hamish seized the poker and prodded the smouldering peat.

She stood up and edged him aside. 'That's not the way to do it. Here!' She picked up a newspaper from an old pile of them beside the fire and spread it tightly over the hearth. 'See?' she said. 'It's catching already. Oh, hell!' The newspaper in her hands suddenly caught fire and she tossed it at the hearth, where the blazing page went right up the chimney.

'You've done it now,' groaned Hamish. 'I'll phone the fire brigade.'

'Don't be silly, man.' She knelt down by the hearth. 'Nothing's going to happen.'

There was a roaring in the chimney, and then a great pile of soot fell on to the fire and sent a cloud of soot over her kneeling figure.

Hamish went into the office and phoned the fire brigade, which was staffed by local volunteers.

'You've neffer seen the like,' said volunteer fireman and crofter Perry Sutherland. 'There was Hamish's boss, black all over. They'd been drinking, too.'

And the gossip flew from house to house. 'He can't leave the women alone, not even his own superior officer,' complained Mrs Wellington on the phone to Angela Brodie. 'They were getting drunk together and that's how the fire started.'

'I don't see –'

'Mark my words, it's the duty of this village to see that our policeman gets respectably married as soon as possible!'

Hamish Macbeth was lucky in that the village women liked nothing better than to enter a bachelor's home and give it a good scrub. The next morning, despite his protests, a squad headed by the Currie sisters descended on him with mops and pails, dusters and brushes, and proceeded to clean every bit of soot out of his living room.

He thanked them profusely even though they kept giving him lectures on the benefits of marriage. He wanted to point out to the

Currie sisters that they themselves had managed very well without getting married, but he feared the remark would hurt.

He left them to it and went out to the waterfront, where filming was in progress.

They had a grand day for it, reflected Hamish. It was cold but clear and the sea loch lay like glass under a pale blue sky with only little wisps of cloud.

He leaned on the sea wall. The action had moved to the shingly beach. The leading actress, Ann King, was being 'raped' by a bearded actor in jeans and a camel coat.

Hamish saw the director, Paul Gibson, running here and there, shouting instructions. The actor who was playing the rapist stopped and shouted, 'Her clothes won't rip.'

'They should rip,' said Paul. 'The costume department were told to make them rippable. Here!'

He strode up to Ann and jerked at the front of her blouse, which tore, revealing two large breasts.

There was a hiss of shock from the village onlookers. Then the minister, Mr Wellington, appeared on the beach.

'Stop,' he cried. 'You will take your filthy, indecent antics elsewhere.'

Someone put a coat over Ann's shoulders as Paul shouted, 'Take a break.' Then he walked off with Mr Wellington.

The actors, cameramen and soundmen made their way up on to the waterfront and disappeared inside a large trailer which served as a cafeteria.

Hamish followed them. He hadn't had breakfast and he felt the lure of free food. Angela Brodie came up to him with Lugs on a leash. 'Take your dog, Hamish. I've got to go to Strathbane.'

Lugs grinned up at Hamish. 'Come on, then,' said Hamish. 'Maybe I'll get you some breakfast as well.'

He entered and queued up at the counter. When it came to his turn, he asked for sausage, bacon and eggs, coffee, and an extra plate of sausages.

Because Hamish was in uniform, the man behind the counter thought he was an actor and dished out his request without a murmur.

Hamish sat down at a table opposite Ann. She was a pretty woman with thick hair dyed as red as Hamish's own. Her eyes looked green because of tinted contact lenses. Bits of her bosom showed through her open coat and torn blouse, but she seemed unaware of the exposure. She watched him with amusement as he blew on the plate of sausages to cool them and then put the plate on the floor for Lugs.

'I didn't know we had a policeman in this scene,' she said.

'I am a policeman,' said Hamish. He held out his hand. 'Hamish Macbeth. And you are Ann King.'

'Do you like the show?'

'Don't really watch it,' said Hamish. 'It's not very representative of life in the Highlands. We don't get that much rape. Are you working on John Heppel's script?'

'Yes. Harry Tarrant says we should do it in his memory. Your food's getting cold.'

Hamish shovelled in two large mouthfuls and then asked, 'You knew John, of course. How did you get on with the great writer?'

'I hardly spoke to him. He was a pain in the neck. He was always walking into the scene and shouting that it wasn't faithful to his script. Paul always had to take him away and soothe him down.'

'Did he have any friends on the cast?'

'Maybe you should speak to Patricia Wheeler. She plays the honest crofter's wife. They went around together.'

'Is she here?'

'No, she's not in this part.'

'Listen up, everybody!' Paul Gibson stood at the entrance. 'We can do the rape scene somewhere else before the locals lynch us. We'll do the walking bits. Ann, I want you back on the beach. The first shots weren't any good. You've to walk along singing to yourself and looking carefree. Cameron, you'll be lurking behind the rocks.'

'There aren't any rocks,' complained the actor who played the rapist.

'Then find something. We'd better get something out of this. The place is crawling with police.'

Hamish feared for the villagers. Heather must have given orders that they were all to be interviewed again.

He finished his breakfast and took Lugs back to the police station, which smelled strongly of carbolic soap and furniture polish. The women had left. He poured Lugs a bowl of water, locked up the station and went back to the waterfront.

How many times did Paul expect Ann to walk along the beach? It seemed as if he was never going to be satisfied. At last he called, 'It's a wrap. Take a break.'

Hamish moved to the top of the steps leading up from the beach and accosted Paul Gibson.

'I would like a word with you,' he said.

'I could do with a drink,' said Paul.

'There's a pub along by the harbour.'

'Good. We'll go there.'

When they were seated, Hamish said, 'You're spending a long time over John's script.'

'Well, we had to put it on one side and do another one last week.'

'But doesn't the storyline follow one episode after another?'

'Yes, but the Heppel script was to be a one-off.'

'Might I see a copy of the script?'

'Why?'

'Might give me a clue.'

'Sally!' called Paul. Sally Quinn, the script editor, who had been standing at the bar, came over to them. 'This copper wants to see a copy of John's script.'

A look passed between them. 'The one we're working on?'

'Sure. John's script. Give him a copy.'

She went back to where she had been standing and picked up a heavy briefcase from the floor and extracted a folder. She took out a script and brought it to Hamish, who thanked her.

He turned back to Paul. 'You said you didn't get on with John.'

'He was very excited about his script. He loved television.'

'I thought the only part of television he loved was getting his face on it,' said Hamish dryly.

'You're unkind. He was difficult, but we all miss him.'

Hamish looked at the director with raised eyebrows. But perhaps John was so enamoured of television that he had behaved himself better than usual.

'Where can I find Patricia Wheeler?' asked Hamish.

'Why?'

'I gather she was friendly with John. You see, he might have said something to her about being frightened of someone who was threatening him.'

'We're moving up to the forecourt at the Tommel Castle Hotel this afternoon. She'll be there. Now, I'd better get back.'

Hamish began to read the script. It seemed very workmanlike. There were none of the pseudo-literary flourishes he would have expected from John.

He left the pub and got into the Land Rover outside the police station. From inside, Lugs gave a peremptory bark. Hamish unlocked the door. 'Okay, you can come.'

He lifted Lugs up into the passenger seat, climbed in and drove off up the road to the Tommel Castle Hotel. He wondered what the film people were using it for. He had only read the first part of the script. No doubt in these politically correct days, the villain would turn out to be some rich laird.

He left Lugs in the Land Rover and went into the manager's office. 'Is that literary agent still here?' he asked.

'He's just arrived back. He keeps coming and going. He's that excited about Alistair Taggart,' said Mr Johnson. 'Hamish, who on earth is going to buy a book in the Gaelic?'

'Beats me. Is he in the hotel?'

'Yes, I'll phone him.'

Hamish walked over to the coffee machine and helped himself to a mug and then slid two biscuits for Lugs into his pocket.

'He's coming down,' said the manager, replacing the receiver. 'He says he'll see you in the bar.'

Clutching the script, Hamish went through to the bar. Blythe Summer walked in. 'What's up?' he asked. 'Nothing wrong with Alistair, is there?'

'No, not that I've heard. Why are you bothering so much about a book in the Gaelic?'

'It'll catch the imagination. You've no idea how many classes in Gaelic there are in Edinburgh and Glasgow. I'm getting it translated. I think I'll get a Booker Prize out of this one.'

'Good luck. I wanted you to look at this script. It's supposed to have been written by John Heppel.'

'Must I? Never could stand either the man or his writing.'

'You knew him?'

'He wanted me to act as his agent. He sent me *Tenement Days*. I thought it was a load of rubbish. But he went ahead and got it published and got an award and then kept sending me nasty letters about how I had turned down Scotland's greatest literary talent. Wait till I get a drink. I'll need a stiff one if I'm going to read anything written by Heppel. What are you having?'

'I've still got some coffee. That'll do me fine.'

Blythe bustled back with a large brandy and soda. He took a sip and then said, 'Here goes.' He took out a pair of glasses and perched them on his nose.

Hamish waited patiently. He looked around. He could remember the days when the hotel was the family home of his ex-fiancée, Priscilla Halburton-Smythe. Her father, the colonel, had fallen on hard times, and Hamish had suggested to him that he turn his home into a hotel. The result was a success for which the colonel gave Hamish no credit at all. His favourite story was how the idea had come to him in a blinding flash.

Blythe cleared his throat and shook his head. 'John Heppel never wrote this.'

'You're sure?'

'Absolutely.'

Chapter Nine

When I am dead, I hope it may be said:
'His sins were scarlet, but his books were read.'
                                        – Hilaire Belloc

Hamish felt quickening excitement. Blythe rustled the papers. 'They probably found they couldn't work with his flowery prose and got someone to tighten it up and cut out all the waffle. This seems a very competent script. What's it all got to do with his murder?'

'I wanted to read the original to get a better feel of the man's character. But why are Paul Gibson and that script editor trying to cover up the fact that they aren't using John's script?'

'Why not ask them?'

'Oh, I will. Here's trouble.'

Heather Meikle walked into the bar. 'What are you doing here, Macbeth?' she demanded. 'I told you to interview the villagers.'

'Police and detectives seemed to be already doing that, ma'am,' said Hamish meekly. 'But there's something interesting here.'

'Really?' She sat down. 'Get me a whisky. A large one.'

'Allow me,' said Blythe, giving Hamish a sympathetic look.

'Who's he?' asked Heather, jerking a thumb at Blythe's broad back as the literary agent walked over to the bar.

'He's a literary agent who hopes to promote a novel written in Gaelic.'

'Then he's daft. So what have you got?'

Hamish told her about Blythe's assessment of the script. 'I don't see the point,' she complained. 'Oh, thanks,' as Blythe handed her a double whisky.

'The point is this,' said Hamish eagerly. 'As they seem to be so anxious to cover up what was in the original script, I'd like to know what it was. The whole atmosphere of this murder is wounded ego. Maybe some actor or actress didn't like the part. No, wait a bit. They wouldn't have the power to change the script. Could we get a search warrant?'

'For Strathbane Television? Their lawyers would take us to the cleaners. Besides, Alice Patty's family are already suing the police.'

'Unless Alice Patty turns out to have been murdered.'

'Dream on.'

'Got the autopsy report yet?'

'Got the autopsy report yet *what*?'

'Sorry. Have you got the autopsy report yet, ma'am?'

'Not yet. Have you anything else?'

'There's an actress due up here soon, Patricia Wheeler. She's said to have been close to John. I wanted a word with her in case John said anything to her that might give us a clue to his murderer.'

'I'll get Anderson to speak to her.'

'Hey, wait a minute,' protested Blythe. 'Why should someone else interview her when it was this officer here who thought of it?'

'Get me another whisky and I'll think about it.'

Blythe rose to his feet. 'Get it yourself, you old bag. I don't work for you.'

Hamish was sorry to see him go. There was something very intimidating about Heather. Hamish had always thought of himself as a truly modern man, treating women like equals. But what about women treating men like equals?

Heather seemed unfazed by the insult. She held out her empty glass to Hamish.

'I don't have any money on me,' lied Hamish.

'Oh, well, I'll get it.' She leaned back in her chair and roared at the barman, 'Another of these?'

Hamish suddenly remembered Lugs. The dog would be dying to be let out by now.

He rose to his feet. 'I'll just see if the television people have arrived.'

'You can get a clear view from the window. Sit down.'

'I've got my dog locked up in the Land Rover.'

To his surprise, she said mildly, 'Go and get it.'

'I will not let that bloody woman intimidate me,' said Hamish to his dog as he lifted Lugs down from the Land Rover and fished out the two biscuits he had kept for him from his pocket. 'Here's the television lot. I wonder whether I can get rid of her.'

He took out his notebook and searched for Elspeth's mobile phone number. He dialled and waited impatiently until she answered.

'Elspeth, could you do something for me?'

'Like what?'

'There's a woman who's replaced Blair, and I want her out of the way for a bit. She's in the bar at the Tommel Castle Hotel. Could you phone her and ask her if you could interview her? Woman's angle. All that stuff.'

'I need a trade. Matthew's behaving like an idiot. He's talked the features editor into letting him spend the night on Standing Stones Island. "I Spent Night on Haunted Island" and all that guff.'

'Do this for me. I think I've got an angle.'

'Okay. What's this woman detective like?'

'Very charming. You'll get on like a house on fire.'

'Bad choice of words. I believe the police station was nearly in flames last night.'

'Just a chimney fire. Please, Elspeth.'

'Oh, all right. I'll phone her now.'

Hamish walked Lugs around the car park between the newly arrived television vans and then went into the hotel.

He could see Heather talking on the phone in the office. He waited patiently until she came out.

'I'm meeting some reporter down in the village,' she said. 'She wants to do a profile of me. Look, carry on here. I won't be long.'

Hamish took Lugs out for another walk and then put the dog back in the Land Rover.

He asked one of the technicians if Patricia Wheeler had arrived. 'I think I saw her going in for a coffee,' he said.

Hamish went to the mobile cafeteria. He saw Ann King and asked her which of the actors present was Patricia Wheeler. 'That's her over in the corner. Good luck!'

Hamish judged Patricia Wheeler to be in her fifties. She was in the costume of a crofter's wife – or rather what the television costume department fondly imagined the dress of a crofter's wife to be. She was wearing a rough wool grey dress and had a tartan shawl wrapped around her shoulders. Her face was heavily made up. Her grey hair was tied up in

167

a scarf. She had a heavy jaw and small piggy eyes and yet managed to exude an air of strong sexuality.

'Patricia Wheeler? I'm the local constable, Hamish Macbeth. I'd like to ask you a few questions.'

'Sit down. Go ahead.' Her voice was throaty.

Hamish removed his cap and sat down. 'Places everyone!' shouted a girl from the doorway. The actors began to shuffle to their feet.

'That's not for me. Not yet,' said Patricia.

'Were you friendly with John Heppel?'

'Yes, I was. Poor John.'

'Did he mention any enemies he might have made?'

'Only the villagers. He phoned me the afternoon before he was murdered and said they were out to lynch him.'

I don't want to hear this, thought Hamish, assailed again by a pang of doubt that in his efforts to find any culprit other than one of the villagers, he was looking in the wrong direction.

'Anyone else? Anyone in this soap?'

'Not really. He complained a bit about changes to the script, but Paul always managed to calm him down.'

'Ah, the script. I've seen the one you're working on, and I would swear that it wasn't written by John Heppel.'

'I didn't know you were a literary critic. I've got to go.'

'I would like to see the original script.'

'Then you'll need to ask Sally Quinn.'

But Hamish found that Sally Quinn was in her office in Strathbane. He groaned to himself. Heather would return and would wonder where he was, and if he told her what he was doing, she would no doubt give him a blasting over going off on a wild-goose chase. And yet he was sure there was something wrong about it all. Maybe there had been something in the original script that gave a clue to the murderer.

He left Lugs back at the police station and drove off to Strathbane.

Matthew closed his notebook after what he considered another useless interview. He wanted to do the feature on Standing Stones Island, but Elspeth didn't want to be part of it.

He heard the school bell ringing for the lunch break – or dinner break as it was still called in Lochdubh – and decided to call on Freda. He found her attractive. He found Elspeth more attractive, but Elspeth seemed wrapped up in that odd local copper.

He walked past shrieking children in the playground and went into the small schoolhouse. Freda was in her office, marking exam papers.

'I wonder if I could tempt you to a bit of lunch,' he said.

'I'd love to. But I've brought a sandwich with me and I've still got papers to mark. How are you getting on?'

'Getting nowhere. Elspeth's better at writing up the story of the suicide. I've got the features editor interested in a piece about spending a night on Standing Stones Island.'

'How exciting. I've heard it's haunted. Is Elspeth going with you?'

'No, she says she's not interested.'

Freda thought rapidly. Maybe if she charmed this reporter, Hamish might become interested in her. 'I tell you what,' she said. 'It's nice and dry today. Why don't I go with you?'

'That would be great. It's a bit boring spending a whole night on a haunted island on one's own.'

'You don't expect any ghosts?'

'Not one. But I could write a good piece.'

'How do we get there?'

'I've made some inquiries. There's a chap with a boat who would take us over and then pick us up in the morning.'

'What time would we set out?'

'This evening around eight o'clock. Where will I pick you up?'

'Why don't we have an early meal at the Italian restaurant so we won't get too hungry or have to bother taking a picnic? We'll need lots of warm clothes and sleeping bags.'

'I don't have a sleeping bag.'

'I've got a spare.'

'Good,' said Matthew. 'Dinner's on me. Make it early. I'll meet you in the restaurant at six o'clock.'

An hour later an angry Sally Quinn was saying to Hamish, 'The script you read *is* the original.'

'But Harry Tarrant described John Heppel's script as pure Dostoyevsky. The script I saw was just plain uninspired English.'

'Officer, I will have to put a complaint about you to your superiors. Your job is surely to find out which one of those terrifying villagers killed John. Now, go away before I call security.'

Hamish found Heather waiting for him. 'Look here,' she snapped. 'I have been more than tolerant of your odd behaviour. But your place is here, not running around like some starstruck idiot after television people. I have a list here of people in Lochdubh I want you to call on.'

'Today?' asked Hamish.

'Right now.'

She swept out of the police station, leaving him looking at the names on the list: Freda Garrety, Alistair Taggart, Archie Maclean,

Mrs Wellington, the Currie sisters and Angela Brodie.

He took Lugs out for a walk up the fields at the back so that Heather would not see him. Then he fed the dog and headed out, deciding to call on Angela first.

The doctor's wife was at home. Her kitchen looked more chaotic than usual, with cats prowling all over the place and a computer among the jumble of dirty dishes and cups on the table.

Angela pushed a wisp of hair away from her face. 'It is a mess, Hamish, but I've been busy writing.' Her thin sensitive face was flushed with excitement. 'You see, I had an important visitor.'

'Who would that be?'

'Blythe Summer. Mrs Wellington, bless her tweed socks, told him that I was a talented writer. He asked to see what I'd written. I showed him that short story I wrote for the writing class, and he wants me to expand it into a novel. I'll make coffee. No, we'll have a drink.' She got down on her knees and opened a cupboard under the sink. 'I think I've got a bottle of sherry we brought back from Cyprus about twelve years ago. Ah, here it is, right behind the rat poison.'

'I hope you're sure you've got the right bottle,' said Hamish. 'I didn't know you had rats.'

'They turned out to be big mice, but I thought they were rats. There!' Angela put a dusty bottle on the table. 'There's a bit of a leak under the kitchen sink and the label's fallen off, but I'm sure it's sherry.'

'That's grand news,' said Hamish, looking uneasily at the bottle.

Angela produced two fine lead-crystal glasses from another cupboard. She poured two generous measures of sherry. Hamish sniffed cautiously at his drink. 'Smells all right. Here's to your success, Angela.'

'Slainte! What brings you? I haven't really got the time to keep looking after that dog of yours.'

'It's my boss. She's given me a list of people to interview, and you're one of them.'

'Why me?'

'Blessed if I know. Anyway, I thought it would be a good idea to call on you in case she's watching. Have you got a minute? I want to run some things by you.'

Angela threw a longing look at the computer but said, 'Okay. Go on.'

Hamish told her as much as he knew. When he had finished, Angela said, 'You said you think he had probably been having an affair with Alice Patty. He was close to this actress Patricia Wheeler. Maybe he had an affair with her or someone else at Strathbane Television. I mean the murderer might be a jealous woman. I think John Heppel enjoyed the power he felt from humiliating people. Just look how rotten he was to everyone at the writing class. Imagine what he would be like if he was breaking off a relationship with some woman.'

'That's a good point.'

'And talking about women, I saw Matthew Campbell and Freda in the Italian restaurant. They were sitting at that table at the window when I went past around six o'clock. Are you going to miss out there?'

'I'm not that interested,' said Hamish huffily.

'What about Elspeth?'

'That iss over and done with!'

'Hamish, don't you ever think it would be nice to be married?'

The malicious highland streak in Hamish rose up. He looked around the messy kitchen. 'Angela, if anyone needs to get married, it iss yourself and Dr Brodie. You need a good woman to do the housework and take care of both of you.'

'That's it. Off you go, Hamish. And don't dare insult my hospitality again. And furthermore, in future, look after your blasted dog yourself.'

'Sorry,' mumbled Hamish miserably. 'But I don't like folks nosing into my private life.'

Angela glared at him and then relented. He looked so forlorn, standing there holding his cap and looking at the floor.

'We'll both forget about it,' she said. 'But I've got to write.'

Hamish then called on the Currie sisters. For the first time ever, neither of them opened the door, but he heard Nessie call, 'It's open.'

They were both seated in front of the computer, avidly reading a website on the Galápagos Islands. Hamish, who had expected to be besieged by calls from villagers wanting help with their computers, had been puzzled and then relieved when he was left alone.

He walked over and stood behind them. 'You seem to have got the hang of the Internet,' he said.

'It was Angus Petrie,' said Nessie, her eyes still on the screen. 'He shouldn't be in forestry. He's a grand computer teacher. Knows everything about computers.'

Does he now? thought Hamish with quickening interest. 'He boards with Mrs Dunne, doesn't he?'

'Yes,' said Jessie. 'What do you want? We're busy, busy.'

'I'll call again,' said Hamish.

He went out and made his way to Sea View, Mrs Dunne's boarding house.

When she answered the door, he asked, 'Is Angus home?'

'No, he's not back yet.'

'Do you mind if I wait in his room?'

'I suppose it's all right, you being the police and all. He's not in trouble, is he?'

'No, no, just general inquiries.'

'His room's number 3 off the first landing. It's not locked. I tell my guests to leave their doors unlocked so I can clean.'

'Thanks, I'll find my way.'

Hamish went up the stairs and opened the door of number 3. The room looked bleak when he switched on the light. There was a narrow bed against the wall covered in a pink shiny quilt. A wash-hand basin stood in one corner and beside it a chest of drawers. In the middle of the floor was a wooden table flanked by two upright chairs. A curtained recess in one wall acted as a wardrobe. There was a two-bar electric fire on the hearth with a coin meter beside it.

Hamish sat down on one of the chairs and looked around the room. He would have liked to search the place, but he didn't have a warrant and Angus might walk in on him.

The room was cold. He fished in his pocket and found a fifty-pence piece. He got up and walked over to the meter, popped the coin in, and clicked the dial. Hamish was about to straighten up when he saw two loose floorboards. They looked as if they had recently been prised up. Burning curiosity overcame him. He slipped on a pair of gloves and took out a Swiss knife. He lifted out the floorboards and then shone his torch down into the cavity.

The torch lit up a portable computer, a Toshiba – and John Heppel had used a Toshiba.

Hamish slowly retreated and sat down. He should phone Strathbane at once. But his search had been illegal. He heard a light footstep outside, and then the door opened.

Angus looked at Hamish, and then his eye fell on the space in the floor where Hamish had dislodged the boards.

'Unless you've got one damn good explanation,' said Hamish quietly, 'I think I might have to arrest you for theft and assault. And that's for a start.'

'You'll never believe me.' Angus sat down on the bed and began to cry.

Hamish waited impassively until he had recovered and said, 'Try me.'

Angus gulped and then said, 'It was after the murder. I had a day off and I thought I'd play detective and have a look around the cottage and see if I could find anything. You see, I knew you'd been good about keeping quiet about us going up there, but I thought it'd come out sooner or later and I wanted to see if there was anything I could find.'

'Wasn't there a policeman on duty?'

'No. I looked in the window and saw the computer. I began to think of taking it. I ran into debt not so long ago and I sold my computer. I thought, the police don't want it; it's sitting there doing nothing. I looked around. There was no one about.'

177

'How did you get in? I mean, surely the place was locked up?'

'I thought he might have a spare key somewhere. I searched in the gutter, which is where most folks leave the spare key, and there it was. I let myself in. I wanted to check my e-mails.'

'Man, there's several cybercafés in Strathbane you could have used.'

'But don't you see? Nobody wanted that one. It was just sitting there.'

'Go on.'

'I read some of my e-mails and then sent some off to friends. But after I left, I kept thinking what a waste of a computer it was.'

'Surely you must have considered you were contemplating committing theft.'

'John Heppel wasnae married, and he hadn't left a will. It would all go to the state.'

'How did you find that out?'

'A policeman told someone in the village, and the news went around.'

'Didn't come as far as me.'

'I thought I'd go back and take it. I hadn't locked the door. So I went back, but I looked in the window first and I saw you there and I panicked. I thought you'd find my e-mails and know I'd been using it and I'd go to prison. There was an empty wine bottle by the door. I just meant to give you a tap on the head, but I hit you harder by mistake. I took the computer and ran.'

'Angus, I am going to have to charge you with assaulting a police officer, theft, removing vital evidence from the scene of a crime, and take you to Strathbane, where no doubt they will charge you with murder as well. Now, did you erase stuff from that computer?'

'No, there was nothing on it.'

'Do you have a criminal record?

Angus hung his head. 'Yes.'

'What for?'

'I was just a lad, fifteen. I hacked into the Ministry of Defence computer system.'

'There was nothing in the press. I would have remembered.'

'It was all hushed up. They didn't want anyone to know how easy I had found it. They took me away somewhere and grilled me for days. By the time they'd finished with me, I swore to God I'd never do anything like that again. I was living in Dumfries at the time. I moved all the way up here and got a job in the forestry.'

Hamish stared at him for a long moment. 'Have you the ability to get into the hard drive of that computer and rescue the files?'

'Yes, but I didn't!'

'Wait a bit. I'm thinking. You can't get on the Internet here. There's no phone in your room.'

'I havenae dared touch the machine since I stole it.'

Hamish was in a quandary. He did not think that Angus had murdered John. But if he took him in for assault and the theft of that computer, he knew Angus might also be charged with the murder. The police would figure that anyone who could attack a policeman must be a murderer as well.

'When the police asked you where you were on the evening of the murder,' asked Hamish, 'what did you say?'

'The truth. I was at the writing class with the others when Perry burst in with the news John was dead.'

'And before that?'

'Here. In this room. I've got an old typewriter. It's over there in the cupboard. I was using that to write.'

'Can Mrs Dunne confirm that?'

'She was out all day, and no one else is staying here at the moment.'

Hamish was silent for a few moments. Then he said, 'I hate you for putting me in the hospital.'

'I'm awfy sorry.'

Hamish took a deep breath. What he was about to suggest could lose him his job and get him charged with police obstruction if it ever came to light.

'Have you any holidays owing?'

'Two weeks.'

'Take them now. I want you to come to the police station and work hard at getting into that hard drive. If you speak about it to anyone, then you are going to go to prison and I am going to lose my job.'

Angus wiped his tear-streaked face with his cuff. 'You'd do that for me?'

'Laddie, if you weren't any use to me, I'd have you off to Strathbane so fast your feet wouldn't touch the ground. I need to know what's in that computer. Pack up a bag in the morning and report to the police station. I'll take the computer. I'll need to put an extra lock on the kitchen door and take away the spare key. Too many people just walk in. I'll put a lock on the office door as well. Don't answer the telephone and don't come out of the office until you're sure I'm alone.'

'Thanks. I don't know how –'

'Oh, just shut up, you daft nerd. Give me the computer.'

Angus went and lifted it out. He wrapped it in a plastic shopping bag. Hamish rose and tucked it under his arm.

'Nine o'clock tomorrow,' he ordered.

Chapter Ten

He thought he saw an Albatross
That fluttered round the lamp:
He looked again and found it was
A penny-postage stamp.
'You'd best be getting home,' he said,
'The nights are very damp.'
              – Lewis Carroll

Matthew felt happy as the small boat they had chartered chugged out through the oily waters of Strathbane docks towards Standing Stones Island. Not for the first time, he wondered why anyone would want to become a policeman. All those dreary interviews, over and over again.

He could see Freda was enjoying herself as well, her pointed face lit up with excitement.

'Thank goodness it's calm,' she shouted to him over the noise of the engine. 'I'm sure it can get very rough out here.'

Huge stars blazed above them. One never notices stars in the city, thought Matthew.

The island loomed up bathed in bright moonlight. It was really just a small rocky hill but with a circle of standing stones on its crest.

'I'll be back for ye in the morning,' said the boatman.

'Don't be late,' urged Freda. 'I've got to be at work at nine.'

Matthew had an uneasy feeling that he shouldn't have paid the whole fare in advance. The boatman was a surly, criminal-looking fellow. What if he didn't come back for them?

Too late now, he thought as he and Freda hoisted rucksacks on to their shoulders and climbed up to the ring of stones, which looked like great black fingers pointing up to the beauty of the night sky.

After they had found a slab of masonry to sit on and were drinking Freda's contribution of coffee and Matthew's of whisky, they chatted about this and that until they fell silent.

Matthew began to wonder what on earth he could write. And then he began to feel uneasy. He had never considered himself oversensitive or imaginative, but he began to feel the island didn't want them there. It was as if dislike were emanating from the very ground.

'I read up on this place,' he said, breaking the silence. 'It used to be joined to the land.'

Freda shivered and edged closer to him. 'It's getting colder.'

'Why don't we get into our sleeping bags and have another drink?' suggested Matthew.

'Good idea.'

They snuggled into their sleeping bags. Matthew could feel that odd dislike strengthening into hatred as he sat beside Freda, wrapped in his sleeping bag. 'Do you feel anything odd?' he asked Freda.

'Like what?'

Matthew gave an uneasy laugh. 'As if this place hates us?'

'There's something creepy,' said Freda. 'What was that?' She clutched Matthew.

'What? What is it?'

'I saw something white out of the corner of my eye.'

'Probably a gull. They never seem to go to sleep.'

'Maybe.'

'Oh, hell.' Matthew took another slug of whisky. 'The wind's getting up.'

Freda looked up at the sky. Long fingers of clouds were beginning to stream across the night sky, obliterating the stars.

I can't write about any of this, thought Matthew. I can't write about feelings. If I write that the island hated us, the news editor will suggest a visit to the nearest rehab.

'Do you think,' said Freda in a trembling voice, 'that it might be a good idea if we just cuddled up together and went to sleep?'

'This stone we're sitting on,' said Matthew, shifting uneasily. 'Do you think it might have been some sort of altar?'

'I tell you what,' said Freda. 'Let's get out of this circle and camp on the beach.'

They struggled out of their sleeping bags and then hauled their belongings down to the beach. Matthew shone his torch and found a flat area of springy turf. 'This'll do. Let's open up the sleeping bags and make a double blanket.'

Soon they lay clasped in each other's arms as close as lovers. That odd feeling of hate had gone.

The area of grass they were lying on was shielded by an outcrop of rock. Lulled by whisky and the sound of the sea, they fell asleep.

Matthew was awakened by Freda shaking his shoulder. 'Wake up!' she hissed. 'Listen!'

They could hear faint cries above the steady throb of an engine. 'If that's a boat, maybe they can take us into Strathbane,' said Freda.

'I'd better have a look first.'

Matthew made his way up to the standing stones. He could see the lights of a large boat of some kind out to sea. He nipped back to Freda. 'I've got some night-vision binoculars in my rucksack.'

'What is it?'

'Nothing supernatural. A ship out to sea.'

Matthew found his binoculars and went back to the standing stones. He focussed the binoculars on the large boat. He now saw a smaller fishing boat riding alongside it, rising and falling on the waves. Packages were being unloaded on to the fishing boat.

Maybe it's drugs, he thought. Maybe I've got a story, after all.

A tap on the shoulder made him yelp with terror. He turned round. 'Freda! You nearly frightened me to death.'

'We're safe!' said Freda excitedly. 'There's a boat on the other side coming out to the island.'

'I think they're drug runners,' said Matthew. 'We've got to get back to our stuff and hide it and ourselves.'

Freda clutched him and whimpered. 'I'm terrified. I want to go home.'

'Shhh! I'll look after you. Come on. We've got to hide our stuff before that other boat gets here.'

They crept down to their sleeping bags and stuffed them back in the rucksacks. 'If we hide behind the standing stones, they won't see us,' said Matthew. 'The wind's gone down a bit, so we'll get off all right in the morning.'

They made their way back to the stone circle. Matthew covered their rucksacks with grass and seaweed. He took out his mobile phone and dialled Elspeth's number.

'I'm on Standing Stones Island,' he said. He told her about the boats. 'I think they're drug running. Tell the police at Strathbane and cover the story from your end.'

Elspeth phoned Hamish Macbeth.

'I may not get to Strathbane in time if that's where they're headed, but I'll call headquarters and they can get the coastguard out,' said Hamish.

Matthew and Freda stood behind one of the pillars and listened. They heard the boat Freda had seen and then the sound of the other boat circling the island to join it.

'Damn,' muttered Matthew. 'I must see what they're doing.'

'Don't leave me,' pleaded Freda.

He gave her a quick kiss. 'Just stay here and you'll be fine.'

He moved from the cover of one stone to another until he was looking down at the half-ruined jetty where they had landed. He raised his binoculars to his eyes. They seemed to be sharing out the packages. He concentrated on them.

Cigarettes!

Well, it wasn't drugs, but it was something.

Freda leaned against a standing stone and wished with all her heart that Matthew would come back. And then she heard weird singing: an eerie chant that rose and fell. Her nerve broke, and she ran to where Matthew was hiding, shouting, 'Help! Help!'

Matthew whirled round. 'Freda, for God's sake, keep your voice down.'

'I heard singing,' she said. 'Awful ghostly singing.'

'One of the men's playing Gaelic tunes on the radio.'

A powerful torch shone on them and a brutal voice ordered, 'Get your hands up!'

Rough hands dragged them down to the jetty. The men all had their faces covered with black ski masks.

'I am a reporter with the *Daily Bugle*,' said Matthew desperately.

The leader, or the man who appeared to be the leader, stepped forward. 'Get them aboard. We'll tip them over the side when we're far enough out.'

Guns were shoved in their backs and they were propelled aboard one of the boats.

They were tied up and placed side by side on the deck. Freda was sobbing with fear.

'Do we weigh them down with something?' a voice asked.

'No, they'll be dead of cold, and they can't swim with their arms and legs tied.'

'Freda,' whispered Matthew, 'if we ever get out of this alive, I'll make it up to you. I can't tell them about the police knowing, or they might just shoot us.'

'They're going to drown us anyway,' wailed Freda.

'Right,' they heard the leader say. 'This is far enough. Throw them over the side.'

Hands dragged them to their feet.

And then one of them shouted, 'Coastguard!'

The boat was suddenly bathed in blinding white light from a helicopter overhead, and across the waves towards them surged two police boats and two coastguard vessels.

'Do we shoot it out, guv?' asked one.

'No, chuck all the guns over the side. Untie that pair. They'll try to do us for attempted murder, but we can all swear we were just trying to frighten them.'

'They got James's boat as well.'

'They can't give us much for running cigarettes. Relax.'

Elspeth and Hamish arrived just as Freda and Matthew were being helped ashore.

Detective Chief Inspector Heather Meikle came driving along the dock. 'Well done, you two. Now, if you will come to police headquarters and make a statement . . .'

'Can Hamish Macbeth take our statements in Lochdubh?' begged Matthew. 'Freda is in shock.'

'Do you want to go to the hospital, Miss Garrety?'

'No,' sobbed Freda. 'I w-want to g-go home.'

'Very well. Macbeth, take them back and send over their statements.'

'Before we go,' said Matthew, 'those bastards are going to say they only threatened to drown us to frighten us, but they did mean to kill us. We heard them.'

'Put it in your statement.'

Freda, Matthew and Elspeth got into the police Land Rover. Hamish had ordered Matthew to leave his car keys with the police, who would drive his car over to the Tommel Castle Hotel in the morning. As they were moving off, Elspeth said, 'Stop at the Highlands Hotel on the road out, Hamish.'

'Why?'

'Freda needs to use the Ladies.' She handed Freda a plastic bag. 'There you go. Clean knickers and jeans.'

'How did you know?' asked Freda.

Elspeth grinned. 'Been there, done that.'

While they waited outside the hotel for Freda, Matthew said, 'I'm glad I've got something to write.'

'You mean Standing Stones Island was a washout?' asked Elspeth.

'It wasn't that. It was an eerie place. I felt . . . This is daft. I felt the island hated us – well, not the island, but the bit in the middle of the standing stones. If I wrote that, they would be asking what I'd been drinking.'

To his surprise, Elspeth said, 'I know what you mean. There are parts of Sutherland where people get weird feelings and even see things. The rock up here is the oldest in the world, and any soil is a very thin covering. I sometimes wonder if in a way it *records* things. But what did you hope to write? I mean, you weren't actually hoping to see a ghost, were you?'

Matthew gave a reluctant laugh. 'I suppose I never really thought beyond the headline. "Reporter Matthew Campbell's Night on the Haunted Island."'

Freda came out and joined them, and Hamish drove off. 'I know you're both tired,' he said, 'but I'd better get your statements as soon as we get back to Lochdubh, and that way you can both have a good night's sleep.'

'All right,' said Matthew, 'but make it quick.'

Before he fell asleep in the safety and comfort of his hotel room, Matthew thought about Freda. He had liked the way she had clung to him. Elspeth would never have done that. He looked forward to seeing her with a feeling of pleasant anticipation.

They had made their statements. He had filed his story, and he knew Elspeth was filing her part in it about her race with Hamish to Strathbane and the activity on the docks.

And to think he had considered the Highlands boring!

* * *

Angus arrived at nine in the morning. Hamish, bleary-eyed, let him in. 'Are you getting a locksmith round?' asked Angus.

'No, I'll change them myself. I meant to do it ages ago, and I've got locks out in the shed. Make some coffee for both of us, and then I'll clear the desk in the office for you. Just in case my boss arrives and wants to go in there, I'll tell her loudly that I've got something wrong with the police computer and you're fixing it for me, and you hide the Heppel one.'

'Okay.'

'I'll clear the desk now and then shave and get my uniform on. I've a feeling the Lady of the Cast-Iron Liver will be here shortly.'

'Drink a lot, does she?'

'Like a fish. Make coffee.'

Hamish moved the police computer to one side of the desk and unlocked the drawer where he had hidden John's laptop, and put it on the desk. Then he showered and shaved and got into his uniform.

He had drunk his coffee, walked and fed Lugs, and changed the locks before Heather arrived. He had hoped the excitement of catching the cigarette smugglers might have kept her away a bit longer, but there she was, rattling at the handle of the locked kitchen door.

He unlocked it and let her in.

'That was good work,' she said, shrugging off her coat and handing it to him. 'Some members of that gang have been in prison already for running drugs. But cigarettes are so expensive in this country that a lot of the drug dealers have gone over to smuggling cigarettes. But that's not why I'm here. The toxicology report revealed that Patty's body contained traces of a heavy narcotic. Also, there's now some forensic gobbledygook, which comes down to the fact that she could not have slit her wrists herself. There is no report from the computer expert in Glasgow yet. So I'm off back to Inverness. Got any whisky?'

Hamish glanced at the clock. It was eleven in the morning. He lifted down a bottle from the cupboard and a glass and put both on the table.

'Why are you leaving for Inverness, ma'am?'

'I'm not needed any more. Blair's suspension has been cancelled. Now it has been established that Alice Patty was murdered and not driven to suicide, he's been exonerated. It's a pity. We could have made a good team, Hamish.'

More like master and servant, thought Hamish.

'Would you consider a move to Inverness?'

'It's kind of you to suggest it, ma'am, but I'm more use here.'

She drained her glass and poured herself another hefty measure. Hamish watched the diminishing whisky sourly. I've a good mind to put another bottle on my expenses and say it was for entertaining her, he thought.

She drained that glass and stood up. 'Coat!'

Hamish fetched her coat and helped her into it. 'Well, I'm off,' said Heather. She kissed him on the cheek. 'Be seeing you.'

'I don't know which one is worse,' said Hamish to Lugs after she had gone, 'her or Blair.'

Then he realized with a feeling of intense relief that the murder of Alice Patty would shift the focus away from the village.

The phone in the office rang. Hamish unlocked the door, shouting, 'Don't answer that.'

'I wasn't going to,' muttered Angus.

Hamish picked up the phone. Blair's guttural Glasgow accent sounded down the line. 'Get out there and interview that lot in the village.'

'But surely the murder of Alice Patty means that one of the television people is probably the culprit?'

'I mean the television lot, you stupid teuchter. Haven't you poked your nose outside that police station of yours? They're filming there today. Jimmy Anderson and some police are there already. I'm too busy winding up a smuggling racket I exposed.'

'If you look at your records, sir,' said Hamish gleefully, 'I was the one who reported it.'

'Just get to work, you lazy bastard!'

* * *

195

Some of the villagers were baffled that day by the new lock on the police station door. It had become a handy place from which to borrow things, like a can opener or a carving knife.

Hamish did not know this and was occasionally puzzled by missing items which would suddenly reappear a few days later.

Hamish went out and found the television vans and equipment along the waterfront.

He leaned on the wall and looked down on the beach. He was joined by Jimmy Anderson. 'Heard the news?' asked Jimmy.

'Aye.'

'It means we've got Blair back, and old Iron Knickers has gone back to Inverness.'

'I know. She was here this morning.'

'You'd best watch out, Hamish. She was singing your praises.'

'Oh, well, she's gone. That's that.'

'Don't be too sure.'

'Why?'

'There was a buzz about two years ago that some good-looking copper was trying to accuse her of sexual harassment. Of course, it was all hushed up and the young copper was promptly transferred to a station in the Outer Hebrides.'

'You know, maybe I should get a spyhole for that kitchen door. Then I'd know who was out there. People just drop in and out as if it's some sort of hotel. Now, I think we should start with Patricia Wheeler. She was close to

John Heppel. I tried her yesterday. Angela Brodie's come up with the idea that maybe we should be looking for a murderess. I'm pretty sure Heppel was having an affair with Alice Patty. Who knows what other women he was messing around with. Then there's another thing: the script they're using and saying was John Heppel's bears no relation to his writing.'

'Doesn't that usually happen?'

'What do you mean?'

'I had a lady friend once who wrote scripts for some hospital series. She wrote draft after draft and still they asked for another. By the time they were demanding a fourteenth draft, she cracked and took the first draft out of the bottom of the pile and sent them that. They said great, we'll use it. But she said what appears on the screen usually bears no relation to the original script.'

Hamish gave a disappointed 'Oh.' He thought of Angus working away at the computer and the great risk he had taken in not reporting the young man.

'Is it just you and me?' asked Hamish. 'Blair said he was sending a lot of police over with you to cover the television people.'

'Aye, but he's decided we should go it alone because he thinks one of the locals nicked that computer of Heppel's. They're all over in Cnothan going from house to house with search warrants. If they can't find anything there, they'll start on Lochdubh.'

'I hope they don't come around the police station.'

'Why?'

'I don't want them messing up the police computer.'

'They'd hardly do that. Thon computer's a big beast and they're looking for a laptop. Is that a rape going on?'

'Supposed to be,' said Hamish, 'except it's a fully clothed one. Mr Wellington, the minister, objected to her having her clothes ripped off.'

Jimmy shook his head in wonderment. 'The things actresses go through. He's got her head in a puddle.'

'Let's go to their café,' said Hamish, 'and start with the people there. I hope Patricia's one of them.'

Patricia Wheeler was found sitting at a table on her own. She scowled when Hamish and Jimmy sat down opposite her. 'I've already spoken to you,' she said, looking at Hamish.

'We've just discovered that Alice Patty was murdered,' said Jimmy.

Her face blanched under her make-up. 'That can't be true. She slit her wrists.'

'Aye, well, someone drugged her first and cut them for her. Now, was John Heppel having an affair with her?'

'I don't know,' said Patricia. 'I mean, she did haunt him. She was always turning up on location and bringing him sandwiches and coffee and hovering around him. He was charming to her, I'll say that, which is more than . . .'

She bit her lip.

'What you're trying to say,' said Hamish, 'is that Heppel was usually rude and nasty to everyone.'

'No, I'm not saying that at all. John was a dear and I'll miss him.'

'Did you have an affair with him?' asked Hamish.

'Of course not.'

'It's best to tell the truth. We can find out, you know, sooner or later.'

'Well, we did have a bit of a fling. Things like that happen in show business. Here today, gone tomorrow.'

'Who else was he screwing?' asked Jimmy bluntly. 'Apart from you and Alice Patty.'

'I don't like your tone. No one, as far as I know.'

'Who ended your affair?' asked Hamish.

'It just burned out. We remained friends.'

'Did he dump you for Alice Patty, or was it the other way round?'

She got to her feet. 'I find your questions offensive. Next time you want to speak to me, call my lawyer!'

Patricia stormed out.

Jimmy shook his head. 'I'll never understand women. By all accounts, Heppel was a bully and a bore and yet he managed to get his leg over.'

'Would you have even considered an affair with a woman like Alice Patty?' asked Hamish.

'God, no. That awful refeened accent. Mind you, I wouldn't mind having a go at our Patricia. Still, let's split up and talk to the luvvies. Give it two hours and I'll meet you in the pub unless you've got anything at the station.'

'Not a drop. Herself finished it off this morning.'

When they met up in the pub two hours later, both Hamish and Jimmy were feeling depressed. 'Did you get the same guff?' asked Jimmy. 'Everybody loved everyone else and they're all one big happy family and they all just *adored* John Heppel.'

'Pretty much.'

'I've been thinking,' said Jimmy. 'There's one connection between the village and Strathbane Television.'

'What's that?'

'Alistair Taggart.'

'No. He's been cleared, surely, and Heppel was murdered before Alistair had anything to do with television.'

'Think about it. Heppel had insulted him. He's got a violent temper. He drinks.'

'Like you,' said Hamish as Jimmy downed his second whisky.

'Not like me. I'm as calm as a lamb. He went

on television after Blair released him. He could have met Patty then.'

'He was at the writing class.'

'Can't pinpoint the exact time of death. You know that, Hamish. He could have gone back there again, just before the class, and killed him.'

'He was sober at the class. Anyway, he's more likely to have beaten John to death than to mess around with naphthalene. He uses a typewriter. I don't think he'd know one end of a computer from another.'

'I'm going to have a talk to him. Want to come?'

'No, I'm going back to talk to the television people. I mean, Jimmy, if the script had been changed through several drafts, why didn't they say so?'

'I gather this episode of *Down in the Glen* is to be featured as an in memoriam to Heppel. They're not going to turn around and say most of it wasn't his writing.'

'You've got a damn answer for everything,' said Hamish crossly. 'See you later.'

When Hamish emerged, it was to find the vans had gone. The day had that white light it always gets in the Highlands just before darkness falls. He guessed they'd probably moved back to the Tommel Castle Hotel.

He collected his dog and drove off.

Chapter Eleven

All the world's a stage, but some of the players have been very badly miscast.
— Oscar Wilde

Hamish diligently questioned members of the cast, technicians, make-up girls, and actors for the rest of the day without managing to make a crack in their statements of goodwill to all.

Perhaps away from the location, he might have better luck. Surely there was some typist or gofer or some sort of menial who might be able to give him a different picture.

He joined up with Jimmy and outlined his plan. 'I'll run it past Blair first,' Jimmy said.

'Must you?'

'I'll put it up as my idea and you can come along. If I say it's your idea, you know what he's like: he'll tell you to go back to your local duties.'

Jimmy walked away and phoned. He came back with a grin on his face.

'Good. I've got his lordship's permission.'

They drove in their separate vehicles to Strathbane after Hamish had left Lugs at the police station. I wish the light days would come back, thought Hamish. It's like living in one long dark tunnel. Were night shots more expensive than day shots? A lot of the filming when he had left seemed to be going ahead, floodlit.

They parked at Strathbane Television and got out. 'I should have told you to wear plain clothes,' said Jimmy. 'It's hard to have a friendly wee chat with a long drip like you in uniform.'

'I've got clothes in the Land Rover, in the back.'

'Put them on.'

Hamish emerged after some minutes, wearing a thick fisherman's jersey and jeans.

'Right now,' said Jimmy, 'we hover on the other side of the road and look for a likely target. What's the time?'

'Coming up to five-thirty.'

'The common folk should be finishing work any minute now.'

Four young women came out, laughing and chattering. 'There we go,' said Jimmy. 'We'll follow them. Let's hope they all go for a drink or a coffee.'

The girls turned in at a pub, and Hamish and Jimmy followed them in.

Hamish heard one of them say, 'Let's take this table. Whose turn is it to buy the drinks?'

'Mine,' said Jimmy, moving in on them.

The girls looked from Jimmy with his foxy face and bright blue eyes to the tall figure of Hamish. 'All right,' said a dark-haired one, tossing her hair in the manner of a shampoo advertisement.

They all ordered alcopops. Jimmy and Hamish went to the bar. 'I think we'd better tell the truth about who we are,' said Hamish as Jimmy paid for the drinks.

'Why?'

'I think they'll find it exciting. I mean, there's now two murders and the press wouldn't bother interviewing secretaries, which is what I think they are.'

'Okay. Let's go.'

When they were seated at the table, Hamish began. 'I'm Police Constable Hamish Macbeth, and this is Detective Inspector Jimmy Anderson. And you are?'

The dark-haired one said she was Kirsty Baxter, and she introduced her friends as Sally Tully, a petite blonde; Kate McCulloch, a thin sallow girl; and Robin Sorrell, a small quiet creature with gelled hair in four colours.

'Are you investigating the murder?' asked Kirsty excitedly.

'Yes, we are,' said Jimmy. 'Are you all secretaries?'

Kirsty said, 'I am and so's Sally. Kate works in the costume department and Robin's a researcher.'

'Did any of you know John Heppel?'

'I did,' said Robin. 'Last time he wanted to go on location up at Betty Hill, I had to go ahead and find a hotel for him. He kept complaining about the service, so I was sent to see what I could do. He seemed very pleasant and asked me to join him for a meal. Then at the end of the meal he suggested we go to his room. I asked why. He leered at me and said, "You know." I told him flat, I'm not that sort of girl. He went apeshit. He said he'd spent money on a meal for me. I pointed out the television company was footing his bills.

'He said he'd have me fired. I thought he was mad. I put in a report of sexual harassment. The big cheese called me in.'

'Harry Tarrant?'

'Yes, him. He told me I didn't understand the artistic temperament. He said great writers were often great womanizers. He told me to ignore it. I didn't want to lose my job, so I did.'

'What about Patricia Wheeler?' asked Hamish. 'She had a fling with him.'

Sally giggled. 'Talking about flings,' she said, 'I was working late one night because there were urgent letters to be typed. I work for Mr Southern, one of the directors. I'd delivered the letters and got them signed. I was making my way to the cloakroom to get my things when a cup of coffee flew past my head and crashed on the wall opposite.

'A door to one of the offices was open and Patricia and John were there and she was screaming at him.' She fell silent.

'What did she say?'

'Can this be off the record, please?' begged Sally.

Jimmy and Hamish exchanged glances. Jimmy nodded.

'She was shouting, "I'll kill you. Who the hell do you think you are to tell me you don't want to see me any more?"

'He said, "Oh, shut up, you old hag. Look on it that I was doing you a favour." She screamed, and then there was the sound of a blow and a crash. Mr Tarrant came along then and said, "Why are you standing there?" I hurried off.'

Kirsty chimed in, 'And next day Alice Patty had a big bouquet of roses on her desk. I took a squint at the card. It said, "Forever yours, John." Don't tell anyone what we said, because Mr Tarrant was a great friend of John's.'

'Did any of you see the script John wrote for *Down in the Glen*?' asked Hamish.

They all shook their heads, but Kirsty said, 'I did overhear Mr Tarrant say that the script was brilliant and it would show people down south that in Scotland we could raise a soap up to literary standards.'

Hamish and Jimmy asked more questions before deciding they had elicited as much information as they were going to get.

They walked out and at Jimmy's insistence went into another pub. 'Maybe we should have taken them over to police headquarters and made it official,' said Jimmy.

'They might just have denied everything.' Hamish looked gloomily down into yet another glass of tonic water. He was getting sick of the stuff. He thought about Angus at the police station. 'I suppose it's easy for an expert to recover material from the hard drive of a computer.'

'They got some sort of forensic hard drive detection machine down in Glasgow. They just plug the hard drive into it, download the stuff on to a disk, put it into another machine, and the contents come up on a screen.'

'But an amateur could do it?'

'Don't ask me.'

'Got to go.' Hamish dashed out of the pub, leaving Jimmy staring after him.

He drove fast all the way to Lochdubh. He parked at the police station. The door was locked. He fumbled with his new ring of keys until he got the right ones and unlocked the door.

The door to the police office was standing open. There was no sign of Angus and, worse than that, no sign of John Heppel's computer.

He rushed along the waterfront to Sea View. Mrs Dunne said that Angus had packed up and left.

'I'm a fool!' said Hamish, and she stared at him in amazement.

It was only when he was walking back to the police station that he realized there had been no welcome from Lugs. With a feeling of dread in the pit of his stomach, he went back into the police station calling for his dog. No Lugs.

Angus didn't have a car. Angus would have to have taken the bus.

Hamish drove back to Strathbane with the siren on and the blue light flashing. He went straight to the bus station. He questioned the clerk at the ticket office and was told that a young man with a dog had booked a ticket on the Inverness bus.

He headed off for Inverness. Angus knew that Hamish could not report him to the police.

In Inverness he checked first at the bus station and found that so far no one of Angus's description had been booked on a Glasgow or Edinburgh bus. He then called at bed and breakfasts, one after the other, without success, until he remembered there was a YMCA.

The man who ran the hostel said that someone of Angus's description with a dog had called in looking for a room about half an hour ago. He told him they couldn't take the dog as well.

He might be walking the streets, thought Hamish, running back to where he had parked the Land Rover.

* * *

209

'Come on, Lugs!' said Angus, dragging on the leash. He had taken a great liking to Lugs and had got the dog to come with him by saying, 'We're going to see Hamish,' something that Lugs had seemed to understand. Now the dog kept sitting down and looking at him balefully out of those odd blue eyes of his.

'I'm going to leave you,' said Angus furiously. He dropped the leash and walked on. Lugs stared after him and then pricked up his huge ears. Just as the police Land Rover rounded the corner of the street, Lugs darted forward and sank his teeth into Angus's trousers.

'Get off!' howled Angus. There was a tearing sound as the seat of his trousers came away in Lugs's teeth.

The next thing Angus knew, a furious Hamish Macbeth was climbing down from the Land Rover. Angus began to run, but Hamish, who had won cups for cross-country running, brought him down with a rugby tackle, jerked him to his feet, and shook him till his teeth rattled.

Then he handcuffed him and shoved him in the back of the Land Rover. He tenderly lifted Lugs on to the passenger seat.

'You are going back to Lochdubh,' he shouted at Angus. 'You are going to check back in at Mrs Dunne's and go on as if nothing has happened, or I will beat the pulp out

210

of you. You couldn't get into the hard drive, could you?'

'No,' whimpered Angus.

'Why not?'

'It wasnae my fault. Man, nobody in the country could get into that hard drive. Someone used a programme that doesnae just delete the files but overwrites them with random garbage, maybe seven times.'

'That would take a great deal of computer knowledge, wouldn't it?'

Angus hung his head. 'Not these days. It was originally a U.S. government program, but anyone can buy the software.'

'I can't turn over that computer – you do still have the computer?' asked Hamish.

'Yes.'

'I should never have tried to let you off the hook. When this case is over, get yourself out of Lochdubh. I'll neffer, neffer forgive you for trying to steal my dog. Are your e-mails still on the computer?'

'No, I used that program I was telling you about to delete them.'

'Where did you buy it?'

'I pirated it.'

'So you're a double thief as well as a dog-napper.'

'You're never there,' protested Angus, 'and I thought Lugs liked me.'

'You thought wrong. Now, chust shut your stupid face.'

At Mrs Dunne's Hamish waited until Angus was let in; he had taken off the handcuffs and relieved him of the computer. He went back to the police station and fried liver to give Lugs a generous supper. After he had eaten, an exhausted Lugs fell asleep and began to snore.

Hamish sat at the kitchen table with his head in his hands. He had taken risks before but never one as dangerous or stupid as this.

He rose and pulled down the ladder that led to the loft. He climbed up and hid the computer among all the junk he had stored up there, thinking it might come in useful sometime.

Then he climbed back down and began to pace back and forth. Maybe he was becoming obsessive about that script. Maybe he should be concentrating on Patricia Wheeler. Where did she live? What had she been doing on the night John was murdered?

He sighed. He would go back to interviewing the cast in the morning, and this time he would ask them all where they had been on the night of the murder and take their home addresses.

Matthew Campbell walked out to the forecourt of the Tommel Castle Hotel the following morning. Thanks to Elspeth, their story was coming along nicely. She had suggested they write it like an old-fashioned detective story. Famous writer, quiet highland villages, suspicion and fear.

He took a deep breath of the clear air. Elspeth had introduced him to her old boss, Sam, who ran the *Highland Times*. Somewhere at the back of his mind, Matthew was beginning to wonder what it would be like to be a local reporter in this highland location.

It was a long time since he had felt so energized and healthy. Then there was Freda. He thought about her constantly. They had arranged to have dinner together that evening, and he found his senses tingling in happy anticipation.

Elspeth came out to join him. 'What a lovely day,' said Matthew.

'We don't often get days like this in winter,' said Elspeth. 'What should we do today?'

'Let's see that copper friend of yours and see if he's got anything for us.'

But when they went down to the waterfront, it was to find a preoccupied Hamish, who said, 'I haven't time just now. Maybe talk to you later.'

Elspeth felt crushed. Hamish didn't even seem to see her.

Hamish and Jimmy went doggedly from one television person to another, writing down where each one had been on the evening of the murder and taking down home addresses.

Blair appeared at one point, but for once both Hamish and Jimmy appeared to be working so hard that he didn't have anything to complain about. Police were now searching Lochdubh for John's computer, and Hamish kept thinking uneasily about the computer lying up in the police station loft.

'I think we've got everyone,' said Jimmy at last. 'We should go to Strathbane and check around Patricia's neighbours.'

'I would like to talk to one of those girls again. See if they could maybe get me a copy of the script.'

'Man, you've got that script on the brain. I don't think it's got anything to do with anything. Let's check Patricia Wheeler's address first.'

'Would you mind doing that, Jimmy? I'll meet up with you in that pub next to headquarters at, say, eight.'

'All right. But you're buying.'

Hamish – in his uniform this time – waited across the road from Strathbane Television. Kirsty Baxter, the one who looked like a shampoo advertisement, emerged on her own. Hamish quickly crossed the road and waylaid her.

She looked at him in alarm. 'You promised that what we told you would be off the record.'

'It still is. Can we walk somewhere? I'd like you to do something for me.'

'There's a café round the corner.'

When they were seated over cups of coffee, Hamish said, 'I really would like to see John Heppel's original script. Is there any way you could get it for me?'

'I suppose I could take a look in Sally Quinn's office when she's out. I wouldn't like to get caught.'

'Couldn't you nip in tomorrow when she's in a meeting? Aren't there always meetings in television companies?'

'All the time. But Sally's office is on a different floor. If anyone saw me, they'd ask what I was doing. I could say I was delivering an inter-office memo, but what if they ask to see it?'

'They wouldn't surely ask to see it when it was meant for someone else!'

'Maybe not. Look, I'll give it a try.' She smiled at him and tossed her hair. I wish she wouldn't do that, thought Hamish. 'I think you owe me dinner.'

'Just bring me that script and I'll take you for dinner anywhere you want.'

'I've always wanted to have dinner at the Tommel Castle Hotel.'

'Then I'll take you there.'

* * *

215

Hamish met Jimmy at eight o'clock. 'Get anything?' he asked after telling Jimmy that Kirsty had said she would try to get the script.

'Neighbours confirm that a man of Heppel's description was seen coming and going. I called in at headquarters. A van which sounds like the one seen on the Cnothan Road has been found in the municipal car park. It was stolen a day before the murder. Belongs to a plumber and, yes, he reported it stolen. Forensics have taken it in and they're going over it. But they say it had been cleaned inside and out. Blair's got people checking all the car washes. But back to Patricia. She lives in a block of flats with a private car park. On the day of the murder, in the late afternoon, one of the neighbours saw her get into her car and drive off. Now, she said they'd finished early on location and she'd gone straight home and spent the rest of the day at home.'

'Is she home now?'

'I saw her driving up when I left. I thought we'd go round and see her together.'

Patricia opened her door as far as the chain would allow. 'I'm not talking to you any more without my lawyer,' she said.

'You can talk to us here or talk to us down at the station,' said Jimmy.

She hesitated and then reluctantly unhooked the chain and opened the door wide.

216

The walls of her living room were decorated with photographs of herself in various stage and television productions. The furniture looked as if it came from Ikea. Jimmy and Hamish sat side by side on a white sofa. Patricia sat in an armchair opposite.

Jimmy flipped open his notebook. 'In your statement,' he said, 'you claim that on the day of the murder, you finished on location up on the moors outside Strathbane at four o'clock and went straight home and spent the rest of the evening indoors.'

'Yes, that is true.'

'But one of your neighbours saw you driving off in your car in the late afternoon.'

'He must be mistaken.'

'Come on. Where did you go?'

She gave a well-manufactured start of surprise. 'Oh, how silly. I went out to get a take-away.'

'Where from?'

'Some Chinese place.'

'Which one?'

'I can't remember.'

'We happen to know you went to John Heppel's cottage,' said Hamish.

Jimmy looked at Hamish in surprise, reflecting that one never knew when Hamish Macbeth was lying or telling the truth.

She stared at Hamish for a long moment. Then she gave a shrug. 'So what if I did?'

217

'What if you did!' echoed Jimmy. 'This is looking bad for you. You were at the cottage of a man on the day he was murdered, and yet you lied to the police!'

'I was frightened,' she cried.

'Just tell us what happened,' said Hamish.

She seemed to crumple. 'I just wanted to talk to him,' she said in a low voice. 'That's all. We had been so close. He said he had written in a big part for me. It would have given me a chance to really act. I drove up to the cottage. I got there just before seven o'clock. The lights were on. I hammered on the door but no one answered. His car was there. I tried the door but it was locked. I shouted through the letter box. He didn't answer. So I came away and drove straight home.'

'Was there any other vehicle there?'

'There was a dirty little van parked at the end of the road leading to the cottage. I thought it had been abandoned.'

'Get your coat,' said Jimmy. 'You're going to have to come to headquarters with us now and make an official statement.'

'Have you still got a big part?' asked Hamish.

'No, it was cut.'

'Whose decision was that?'

'Harry Tarrant's.'

'Why was it cut?'

'Paul, the director, said it was because it just didn't work. I wasn't ever one of the main characters, and he wanted to keep it that way.'

At police headquarters Detective Chief Inspector Blair accosted Jimmy and asked him what was going on. His eyes gleamed when Jimmy told him. 'You and I will interview her,' he said. 'Macbeth, get back to your village.'

Elspeth was feeling lonely. Matthew had gone to take Freda to dinner. She decided to go to John Heppel's cottage just to get a feel for the place. The newspaper had given them two more days in case anything else happened. The feature was written, and there didn't seem much more either of them could add to it. Still, the cigarette smuggling story had justified their trip and expenses.

She borrowed one of the hotel cars and set off.

The roaring winds of Sutherland were screeching down from the mountains and whistling through the heather. She drove up to John's cottage, parked and got out. Elspeth remembered her childhood in the Highlands, running before the wind like deer with her friends.

The great oak tree outside the cottage tossed its branches up to the ragged clouds streaming across the sky as if pleading against the ferocity of the wind.

She stood looking at the cottage, dark and secretive. Elspeth suddenly got a feeling she was not alone. There was malice and danger in the air. She got into her car and drove off to the end of the grassy track that led to the cottage, and stopped.

Had it been her imagination? Violence had taken place in that cottage. She thought she had lost her psychic abilities, but maybe they had come back now she was home again. Perhaps all she had sensed was the violence of the murder that had taken place in the cottage. She looked in the rear-view mirror, back along the track to the cottage, and as she did so, she saw a red light at the living room window.

Elspeth reversed, turned and headed back.

Fire!

As she reached the cottage again, the living room window exploded with the heat of the fire, and the wind rushed in, fanning the flames to an inferno.

She pulled out her mobile and dialled the fire brigade. Then she phoned Hamish. She only got the answering machine at the police station, so she phoned his mobile.

'Hamish! John Heppel's cottage is on fire.'

'I'm nearly at Lochdubh,' he said. 'I'll be right there.'

Elspeth got out her camera and photographed the blaze. Then she phoned the

Italian restaurant and told Matthew what had happened.

While she waited for the fire brigade, she watched in fascinated horror as the blaze grew even more ferocious and the roof caved in.

When the fire engine raced up, she moved her car well to the side to give them room.

As the firemen played their hoses on the blaze, Matthew and Freda arrived. Elspeth felt irritated at the sight of Freda. This was a news story, and she didn't like 'civilians' cluttering up the scene. Then Hamish drove up.

Elspeth told him what had happened and about her odd feeling when she was standing outside the cottage.

'Did you smell anything?' asked Hamish.

'Like what?'

'Like petrol.'

'The wind was behind me, so it was probably blowing any smell of petrol away.'

'It must have been deliberate,' said Hamish. 'The murderer must have wondered if he had left any trace.'

'But why now?' asked Matthew. 'Everyone knows the forensics have finished their investigation. Elspeth, do you think you could file the story? Freda and I hadn't finished our meal.'

Elspeth stared at him in surprise. What had happened to hotshot reporter Matthew? But she said, 'All right. You go ahead. I'll go to the

Highland Times and file from there and send the photographs.'

'You're an angel. Come on, Freda.'

'You know what I think?' said Hamish. 'I'm more than ever convinced our murderer is an amateur, and a panicky one at that. I've asked for roadblocks to be set up.'

Hamish then phoned Jimmy and told him what had happened.

'I've just heard,' said Jimmy.

'How did you get on with Patricia?'

'Nowhere. She won't speak without her lawyer. We're waiting for him.'

Hamish fell silent. He was suddenly worried about Angus Petrie. What if Angus were the murderer, after all? Who but the murderer would want that computer? What if it did turn out to be Angus and he was subsequently arrested? The whole story about how Hamish Macbeth had aided and abetted a murderer would not only get him fired, it would land him in court. If only he had not been so focussed on that missing script. It was only a script, after all, but he had become obsessive about finding it. He had, in fact, become so determined to find it was one of the television people, that he might have been overlooking the obvious.

The next morning was damp and drizzly. Hamish took Lugs for an early morning walk along the waterfront. Archie Maclean, the fisherman, was sitting on the harbour wall smoking a roll-up. Hamish wondered, not for the first time, whether Archie ever slept. He was out all night at the fishing but could usually be seen around Lochdubh during the day.

But it transpired Archie had not been out the night before. 'There were the waves out there as high as houses,' said Archie. 'What's this about a fire at that bastard's cottage?'

Hamish told him.

'Probably the fires o' hell where he lives now coming up through the floor,' said Archie.

'I think they'll find out it was set deliberately,' said Hamish.

'It iss like thon thing on the telly.'

'What thing?'

'On *Boys in Blue*.'

'I don't watch it.'

'It wass on the other night. This man murders his wife and makes it look like suicide. He's got an alibi that he was somewhere else. Then he thinks they might find some of his – that stuff.'

'DNA.'

'That stuff. So he sets fire to their flat while the forensic team are working. Kills them all.'

Hamish walked on deep in thought. Surely even an amateur would know that the forensic team had finished their work. But what about someone in television? It was a closed

223

world, where he often thought they lived in their fantasies rather than in the real world.

He returned his dog to the police station. There was an angry message from Blair telling him to get over to Cnothan and try to find an eyewitness to the fire.

Cnothan was his least favourite place, being a drab village bordering on a man-made hydroelectric dam and loch. If only John had lived in the village itself, there might have been the chance of an eyewitness. He drove out on to the moors and to the blackened shell that was John's cottage.

There was a small group of sightseers. He went from one to the other, asking them if they had seen anyone near the cottage the night before, but they all swore they had been nowhere near it. A white-suited forensic team were picking their way through the blackened ruins. The Cnothan fire chief was watching. Hamish approached him. 'Set deliberately?'

'Aye,' said the fire chief. 'They're saying it looks that way. Two petrol cans found out the back.'

Hamish returned to the police station and checked his messages. Nothing from Kirsty. He wondered whether they were still filming at the Tommel Castle Hotel and headed there.

The vans were all parked outside. He went into the manager's office. 'They're all in the lounge,' said Mr Johnson. 'It's evidently the scene where the wicked laird is charged with rape. They've got some Scottish actor trying to do an upper-class English accent.'

'I thought it was only American films where they went in for English-bashing. They want a villain, so they get an English actor.'

'Aye. Did you see *Braveheart*? What a load of bad historical rubbish.'

'Couldn't bear to. Can I take a peek?'

'Go on. Be my guest.'

Hamish walked to the doorway of the lounge and looked in. An actor playing a detective stood in front of the fireplace. He pointed at the laird. 'You followed Morag Mackenzie down to the beach and there you raped her,' he was saying.

'Oh, I say,' said the laird. 'What utter tosh.'

'Cut,' shouted Paul Gibson. He said to the actor who was playing the laird, 'Can you put a bit more life into your voice? You've just been accused of rape. You should be horrified. Right, get set, everyone. Action.'

Hamish moved away and went outside. It was still drizzling, but there was a patch of blue sky over to the west.

He took out his mobile phone and called Jimmy. 'I suppose they've checked everyone's background,' said Hamish. 'Anyone with a criminal record?'

'Minor things. Cannabis smoking. That sort of thing. Nothing major.'

'I wonder if any of them are mad.'

'You mean crazy?'

'Yes, a history of mental disorder.'

'If they have, it wouldn't be on the police files; it would be on their medical records.'

'I think someone really unbalanced is responsible for this. Someone went into a crazy rage and killed John Heppel and then panicked and tried to make it look like suicide. By the way, did forensics ever come up with an explanation as to why they missed taking John Heppel's computer?'

'They keep saying it was black on a black desk. They must have missed it.'

'That's very odd. I mean, there they are, looking for hair and fibres and bits of dust, and they miss a whole computer.'

'I think they're covering up for one of the team. I think it's likely that one of them said he had loaded it up when he hadn't. There's one of them, Jock Ferguson, who's hardly ever sober. He should have been fired long ago, but he's a leading light of the Strathbane police rugby team. Drunk or sober, he plays a grand game and they don't want to lose him. There's an inquiry going on.'

'Right. Talk to you later.'

Hamish drove back to John's cottage. The forensic team were just packing up. 'Which of you is Jock Ferguson?' he asked.

A huge man stepped forward. Hamish could smell whisky on him.

'I want to know why you missed the computer.'

'I'm sick o' this,' said Jock truculently. 'It was an oversight. That's all. We'd checked it for prints and there weren't any and there was nothing on the computer either.'

'But there might have been something on the hard drive.'

'There's an inquiry going on, and I can't stand here all day talking to you.'

Hamish watched him go. He was convinced the man was lying. Had someone bribed him to forget the computer?

He wondered where Jock drank and if he had been seen drinking with any of the television people.

He watched until the forensic team had packed up and left, then phoned Jimmy again. 'I've just spoken to Jock Ferguson, and I'm sure he's lying. I wonder if someone got to him about that computer. Where does he drink?'

'I guess with the rugby boys in the Thistle. It's that pub down Glebe Lane in Strathbane.'

'I know it. I'm going to go there.'

'Hamish, if Blair finds out you've been in Strathbane, there'll be ructions.'

'What happened with Patricia?'

'Grilled for hours but sticks to her story.'

'Has she been charged with obstructing the police?'

'No. Get this: Blair's taken a fancy to her.'

'I didn't think that man took a fancy to anything that didn't come in a bottle.'

'I tell you, he's gone all soppy. And, get this, she's persuaded that director, Paul Gibson, to pay Blair a fee as police adviser. He's starstruck.'

After Hamish had rung off, he climbed back into the Land Rover and headed for Lochdubh, marvelling again at the magic of television. It seemed to be like some sort of drug. People would appear on humiliating game shows just to get in front of the camera.

As he was approaching Strathbane, Elspeth face seemed to appear before him. He really must take her out for dinner and have a chat. He was behaving like a cad by avoiding her.

But his feelings about her were still mixed. Some of the time he felt a sexual longing for her, and at others he felt she threatened his bachelor freedom.

He parked in Strathbane and headed for the Thistle. He went up to the barman and flashed his identification. 'Jock Ferguson drinks in here, doesn't he?'

'Aye, most nights.'

'Have you ever seen him drinking with anyone from Strathbane Television?'

'I watch that soap of theirs, so I would recognize the actors, and I never saw him with one of them.'

'Did you ever see him drinking with anyone who wasn't part of the usual rugby crowd?'

He frowned in thought. Then he said slowly, 'There was one night recently he was in here,

228

and instead of standing at the bar like he usually does, he was over in the corner with a fellow with thick grey hair and a sort of actor's face. Small eyes, squashy nose.'

Paul Gibson, thought Hamish. Could it have been Paul Gibson?

Chapter Twelve

Good Lord, what is man! For as simple he looks,
Do but try to develop his hooks and his crooks,
With his depths and his shallows, his good and his evil,
All in all, he's a problem must puzzle the devil.

– Robert Burns

Hamish phoned back to the police station and checked his messages. There was one from Kirsty. 'I've got it,' she said.

He phoned the television station and asked to speak to her. 'Where can we meet?' he asked.

'You promised me dinner.'

'So I did,' said Hamish. 'I'll meet you at eight o'clock in the Tommel Castle Hotel.'

But when he rang off, his mind was buzzing with the news that it had possibly been Paul Gibson who had been drinking with Jock

Ferguson. Damn! He was slipping. He hadn't asked when. He went back to the Thistle, but the barman couldn't remember the precise evening, only that it had been about a week ago.

Hamish then phoned Elspeth. 'I need your help.'

'Oh, really? I wondered when you were going to deign to talk to me.'

'Come on, Elspeth. I've been that busy. This might turn out to be a big story for you.'

'Where are you?'

'I'm in Strathbane, but I can be at the hotel in half an hour.'

'See you in the bar.'

When Hamish entered the bar, Elspeth was sitting in a corner. She was wearing a tailored trouser suit and a white silk blouse. Her hair was smooth and shiny. Once again, he found himself missing the old Elspeth, who wore dreadful clothes and had frizzy hair. This new Elspeth seemed somehow unapproachable.

'Sit down, Hamish. What gives?'

'For the moment this is off the record,' he cautioned her.

'Okay. Talk.'

He told her about Jock Ferguson and his suspicion that the forensic man had been drinking with Paul Gibson. Her odd silver

232

eyes fixed on his face, Elspeth asked, 'So where do I come in?'

'Gibson's English. I want to get a bit of background on him. Do you think you could tell him you want to write a profile on him and find out what shows he's worked on before? I don't want to pull him in for questioning. If he's our murderer, then he's mad and dangerous.'

'Okay, Sherlock. He's still in the lounge for the great-detective-reveals-all scene. When they break, I'll catch him.'

There was a long silence. Hamish shifted uncomfortably. Then he said, 'I don't know how to handle us, Elspeth.'

'I know. But I've grown out of casual affairs, Hamish.'

'It wasn't a casual affair.'

'But you didn't want to make it permanent?'

'No. I mean, I don't know. If you looked like the old Elspeth, it would be easier to talk. But you look so sophisticated.'

'It's still me underneath.'

'Let me have time to think, Elspeth.'

She looked at him sadly. 'If you need time to think, Hamish Macbeth, then it means you don't want to commit yourself to anything.'

'I'm not saying that. Please, Elspeth.'

'Okay. I'll find out about Paul Gibson. Maybe we'll talk when all this is over.'

'I'd like that.'

Two actors walked into the bar. Elspeth got to her feet. 'They seem to be taking a break,' she said. 'Where will you be?'

'Back at the police station.'

'I'll phone you if I've got something.'

Elspeth went through to the lounge and approached Paul Gibson. 'I'm from the *Daily Bugle*,' she said. 'I wonder if I might interview you.'

'Of course,' he said. 'Now?'

'Yes, now would be fine.'

They sat down in a corner of the lounge. 'What's this?' he said. 'No tape recorder, no notebook?'

'I've a great memory, and I find either of those things puts people off.' Elspeth did actually tape interviews but saw no reason to waste tape on an interview that would never be published, and she did indeed have an excellent memory. 'Just begin at the beginning and go on from there. What attracted you to show business?'

Paul seemed only too happy to talk. He had grown up in the East End of London. His family life had been unhappy. His father had run away when he was very small. He had spent a lot of his time at the cinema. After school he had managed to get a degree in media studies at Luton University and had got a job as a researcher at the BBC. He had pro-

234

gressed to script editor and then director. He had decided to freelance. He described the shows he had directed. There was a production of *Vanity Fair* and then a popular spy series. The spy series had been filmed in 1995. There was a gap until he began to direct a few soap operas starting in 1998, which had all been failures, Elspeth remembered.

'What were you doing between 1995 and 1998?' she asked.

'Oh, this and that,' he said airily. Elspeth did not press him. He said that when Harry Tarrant had phoned his agent and offered the job in the Highlands, he had been delighted to accept. 'I've always been romantic about Scotland,' he enthused.

'Did you have any difficulties with John Heppel's script? I mean, he was hardly a television writer.'

'Oh, I tweaked it a bit. John was happy. We got on just fine.'

Elspeth then let him talk on about himself and his brilliance as a director and finished by taking photographs of him.

Then she went up to her room and typed out everything he had said on her computer, printed it off, and took it down to the police station in Lochdubh.

'This last soap he directed, *Spanish Nights*, it didn't run long, did it?' asked Hamish.

'It was a monumental failure. They even

built a pseudo-village in Spain to use as the setting.'

'But this gap. What was the spy series?'

'It was called *Betrayal*. Filmed by Church Television. They do a lot of programmes for ITV. I'll phone the office in London and see if they've got a contact.'

Hamish went into the kitchen, where he fed Lugs, lit the stove, and put on a kettle of water for coffee. Elspeth was on the phone for half an hour.

She finally joined him, her face flushed with excitement. 'I got through to Church Television. I spoke to one of the producers. He remembers Paul. He was fired from the spy series after the third episode. He had been quarrelling the whole time with the producer, and then he punched him in the face, right on the set, calling him an amateur. He was fired and had a nervous breakdown. The company were very sympathetic. Said he'd been working very hard and it was due to stress.'

Hamish went through to the computer. 'Let me get his statement. Here we are. He says he was back at his digs in Strathbane the whole evening of the murder. I'm going down there to question his neighbours.'

But when Hamish arrived at Paul's address in Strathbane, it was to find that he rented the top half of a villa and that the people downstairs were away on holiday and none of the neighbours had noticed him coming or going.

He went back to Lochdubh, walked Lugs, and changed into his one good suit, then went to the hotel to meet Kirsty.

Her first words were, 'Aren't we going to get a drink at the bar first?'

'We'll have one at the table,' said Hamish. He wanted to make the evening as short as possible so that he could study that script at his leisure.

She was wearing a skimpy top, which showed her bare midriff, and low-slung velvet trousers. She had a small diamond in her navel.

Hamish was glad that there was a new maître d' at the hotel to replace the Halburton-Smythes' former butler, who had once filled that post. He had always sneered at Hamish.

There was a set menu, but Kirsty went straight to the à la carte. She ordered a lobster cocktail, to be followed by fillet steak. 'I think we should have a bottle of white wine to start,' she said brightly, 'and one of these nice reds to follow.'

'Aren't you driving?'

'I took a minicab, and if you're a good boy, I'll let you drive me home.'

Hamish thought of his meagre bank balance. He ordered the set meal for himself. Kirsty ordered the wine. As Hamish would be driving, she drank most of it herself. She said, 'You can look at the script later. This is my evening.'

And she chattered. She talked about her hair shampoo and about how she hoped to be a model. She talked about her diet – not much in evidence, thought Hamish sourly. She talked about her friends and their love life and somehow managed to drink and eat at the same time.

Hamish excused himself and said he had to go to the toilet. Instead, he signalled to the maître d', who followed him out of the dining room. 'Peter,' said Hamish desperately, 'I havenae enough money with me.'

'Tell you what,' said Peter. 'I'll say the bill's on your account and you can make some arrangement with Mr Johnson tomorrow when he comes on duty.'

'Thanks.'

'That's going to be one very drunk young lady.'

'I know.'

Hamish returned to the table. Kirsty continued to drink and eat. Her voice became more slurred, and she began to press her foot against Hamish's under the table. He jerked his chair back. She tried to take his hand. He pretended not to notice and put his hands on his lap.

She finished her meal with a confection of strawberries, cream and meringue, washed down with a half bottle of dessert wine.

'Now let's see that script,' said Hamish over coffee.

Kirsty waggled a finger at him and giggled. 'Not yet.'

At the end of the meal Hamish had to help the staggering Kirsty out to the car park. She draped her arms around him and tried to kiss him, but he disengaged himself and helped her into the police Land Rover.

As he drove off, to his immense relief she fell asleep. He drove gently a little way and stopped. He reached across her to where she had put her briefcase on the floor and gently extracted the script in its green folder and put it in the side pocket of the Land Rover. Then he sped off, driving as fast as possible to Strathbane. On the outskirts he woke her up and asked for directions.

Outside the block of flats where she lived, he helped her down. 'Come in for a coffee,' she said.

'Sorry, I've got to get back.'

'No coffee, no script.'

Hamish helped her up to the front door of the flats. Then he turned and sprinted back to the Land Rover, jumped in and drove off, leaving her staring blearily after him.

Hamish told a protesting Lugs he would need to walk himself, let the dog out, and went into the police office, opened the script and began to read.

The opening said:

Wide shot. The village lies by the sea loch hiding its ancient Gaelic secrets behind closed doors. It is winter and during the long dark nights passions build up and old enmities fester. As Alphonse Karr so rightly put it, 'Plus ça change, plus c'est la même chose.'

ANNIE MACKENZIE and the laird walk along the street. Cut into tight close-up, then track and pan to the door of the pub.

Hamish frowned. He wished he knew more about scripts.

Lugs came in and sulkily slumped down at his master's feet with a sigh. Hamish read on. How had Paul Gibson felt, he wondered, being asked to direct this flowery script where the author stated what camera angles he wanted as well?

He phoned the hotel and asked to speak to Elspeth. 'Hamish, it's after midnight,' she protested.

'I have the script. I could do with your help.'

'Oh, well, I'm awake now. Bring it up.'

'Can I bring Lugs?'

'Why not? The hotel allows dogs.'

Lugs pranced happily out to the Land Rover and waited, with his ridiculous plume of a tail wagging, to be lifted in.

* * *

Elspeth opened her room door to them. She was wrapped in a dressing gown and her hair was tousled. Hamish felt a surge of the old desire, but her eyes were on the script under his arm.

'Come in,' she said. 'Sit down and let's have a look.'

She took the script from him and began to read. Hamish waited patiently. At last she put the script down on her lap and stared at him. 'Harry Tarrant must be a right fool. This is rubbish.'

'You see,' said Hamish eagerly, 'what I'm thinking is this. We've got a director who's had a nervous breakdown, recovered, but been associated with failures. *Down in the Glen* has a big audience. He may have seen it as his chance. Then he gets this script. Do you know any television directors?'

'I know an up-and-coming one on Scottish Television. I think I've got his number in my book.'

'Phone him now!'

'Don't be daft. At this time of night?'

Elspeth reluctantly got the number and phoned. Hamish heard her asking for a Willie Thompson. Then he heard her say, 'In Inverness? Which hotel? Right. Sorry to wake you.'

'He's in Inverness filming a documentary on the new highland prosperity.'

'What's that, I wonder?' said Hamish, thinking of the dinner bill.

'He's at the Caledonian Hotel.'

'I'll get down there first thing in the morning.'

'I'll come with you. I'm not doing anything else, and Matthew is besotted with Freda and seems to have lost interest.'

'Can we go in your car? I took a risk driving the girl I got the script from back to Strathbane, and I don't want Blair to see me on the road.'

'I don't have my car. Matthew drove. I'll take one of the hotel cars. What time? It'd better be early.'

'Seven in the morning?'

Elspeth groaned. 'Right you are, copper. I'll pick you up.'

'Do you have to bring your dog?' demanded Elspeth the following morning as Hamish lifted Lugs into the back seat.

'He's never any trouble, Elspeth.'

'That's why you'll never get married,' said Elspeth, driving off. 'You're married to your dog.'

'You can be a nasty bitch at times,' snapped Hamish, and they drove most of the way to Inverness in cold silence.

At the Caledonian Hotel they found Willie Thompson in the dining room, having breakfast.

Hamish told him that they wanted an expert

to look at a television script and judge how a director would react. 'You only need to read a few pages,' he pleaded.

Willie, a small man with a beard and moustache, sighed, adjusted his rimless spectacles, and began to read.

At last he said, 'I've read enough. Who's directing this?'

'Paul Gibson.'

'What! Paranoid Paul?'

'You know him?'

'I know his reputation. But this script would drive me mad. Who does this writer think he is telling the director which camera angles to use? And what's all this crap about the village? How's he supposed to film that? How on earth did Strathbane Television ever accept a script like this?'

'The boss, Harry Tarrant,' said Hamish, 'was a friend of John Heppel.'

'Oh, the one that got murdered? After seeing this script, I'm not surprised.'

'Harry Tarrant compared it to Dostoyevsky.'

'The curse of directors of soaps is the Dostoyevsky script. Along comes some flowery, literary writer. The bosses are tired of people sneering at their soaps as dumbing down and trash, so they seize on some literary crap and think, that'll show the critics.'

'You've been a great help,' said Hamish. 'Please don't tell anyone about this.'

'I know what you're thinking,' said Willie, 'but you're wrong. Paul Gibson may be a flake, but murder?'

'I never said he was a murderer,' said Hamish.

'So what do you do now?' asked Elspeth on the road back. 'You're never going to get a search warrant on the strength of this script.'

'I'll think of something. Do you mind if we stop here for a bit? I've got to walk Lugs.'

'Oh, *Hamish!*'

Hamish went back to the police station, made himself coffee and sat down to think out a plan of action.

Then he began to wonder if Harry Tarrant, the executive drama producer, knew that the script had been changed.

Leaving Lugs this time after he had fed him, he drove off to Strathbane. The wind had shifted round to the north. He rolled down the window and sniffed. He could smell snow in the air.

At Strathbane Television he had to wait some time before he was able to see Harry Tarrant.

Hamish handed over the script. 'Someone sent me the original script,' he said. 'I wondered whether you knew that they were working on a different script.'

'Nonsense.'

'I've seen the script they're working on. The storyline is vaguely the same, but that's all.'

Harry picked up the phone and dialled an extension. 'Sally,' he said, 'could you step along to my office?'

He turned to Hamish. 'We'll get this sorted out.'

Sally Quinn came in and stopped short at the sight of the script on Harry's desk.

'This copper,' said Harry, 'says you aren't working from John's script.'

'Well, we are, more or less,' said Sally, looking flustered. 'John's script as it stood was unworkable.'

'Why wasn't I consulted?'

'We didn't want to bother you. Paul said a few minor changes were necessary.'

'Bring me a copy of the script he's using.'

Sally glared at Hamish as she went out.

Paul Gibson was still in bed when the maid came in to clean his room. 'Sorry, sir,' she said, backing out. 'I'm that used to you being up early.'

'It's all right. Come in. We're having a late start.'

He climbed out of bed and put on his dressing gown. The maid approached the bed with clean sheets. 'It looks like snow,' she said.

'That's all right. Some snow scenes might be nice.'

'It's that exciting having the telly people here, sir.'

'Must be a very quiet life up here for you,' said Paul, lighting a cigarette.

'Not always. Our local policeman has solved some murders, and we had the telly and newspapers all over the village.'

Paul stiffened. 'If he's that good, why is he still a village bobby?'

'He says he likes it here, that's why. Of course, we're all saying in the village he should get married and settled down. We thought he might marry the schoolteacher, but she's running around with that reporter from Glasgow. Mind you, Elspeth Grant is back. She's a reporter, too, but she and Hamish were sweet on one another. Maybe something'll come of that. Mind if I vacuum, sir?'

Harry glared at the script Sally had just handed him. 'What the hell's the meaning of this?' he roared.

'Paul rewrote it to make it something he could work with.'

'Without telling me?' He buzzed his secretary. 'Get me Paul Gibson on the phone. And get me that director, Johnny Fremont, who did some of the last shows and get him up here fast.'

He turned to Hamish. 'Is there anything else?'

'Why did you choose Paul Gibson?'

'John recommended him.'

'So John Heppel knew him? When? Where?'

'I think he had written to John once wanting to dramatize his book. Paul wrote the occasional script as well.'

The phone rang and Harry picked it up. 'Paul. You're fired.'

Hamish would have liked to hear the rest of the conversation, but Harry waved him away.

Hamish went out into a changed world. The grimy streets and buildings of Strathbane were covered in snow. Fine white snow blew horizontally across the car park.

He drove up on to the moors, driving slowly and carefully because the road ahead seemed to be gradually disappearing. Then he dimly saw the orange light of a snowplough in his rear-view mirror and pulled aside to let it pass. With a feeling of relief, he followed it as far as the Tommel Castle Hotel and swung off into the hotel car park.

Paul Gibson would be rattled at being fired. Hamish decided to interview him and see if he could get him to betray himself.

The television crew were trapped in the hotel because of the blizzard. Mr Johnson came out to greet Hamish. 'My guests are getting fed up with this lot,' he said. 'At first they found it all very exciting, but now they're complaining. Television people do swear a lot. It's like living on a building site.'

'Is the director around?'

'You'll find him in the games room. He was shouting and swearing. I told him I'd turn him out, snow or no snow, so he went in there, the last I saw of him.'

Hamish pushed open the door of the games room, originally the billiard room in the days when the castle had been a private home. The old billiard table was still there, but a table tennis table had been added, and shelves held board games such as Monopoly and Scrabble.

Paul Gibson was slumped in an armchair by the fireplace.

'What do you want?' he asked harshly as Hamish put his peaked hat on the billiard table and sat down opposite him.

'I want to ask you again where you were on the night John Heppel was murdered.'

'Minding my own business, and I suggest you do the same.'

'You hated his script,' said Hamish. 'Harry Tarrant was not aware until today that you weren't using John's script.'

Paul's eyes blazed hatred. 'You! You told him. Why? What's it got to do with a murder?'

'I think it's got everything to do with the murder. You stole that van. I don't think the police have yet looked thoroughly into your background, but if you had the know-how to

248

hot-wire that van, I'll swear that you were in trouble with the law sometime in your past. You knew that as long as John was alive, he'd make sure you stuck to his script. You went up there and somehow forced him to drink a concoction of naphthalene. You watched him die. When he finally did, your hatred wasn't even abated. You poured ink into his mouth.

'Then you panicked. You cleaned up the vomit and scrubbed the floor. You wiped John's face clean where the ink had run down his chin. Then you wiped out the computer files, and just to be sure, you put in some software that would overwrite everything on the hard disk. Maybe you'd never used that program before, and you knew the forensic team would be back the morning after the murder to continue their search. I don't know how you got hold of Jock Ferguson. But you persuaded him to forget about the computer so that maybe you could go back and get it. Did you promise him a part in the soap or something? But you were too frightened to go back.

'You must have had some uneasy moments when you heard the computer had gone missing and the police were searching for it.

'I think that before the murder you had threatened John Heppel, and I think Alice Patty knew about it and said she was going to the police. So you killed her and faked another suicide.'

249

Paul studied him in silence, his eyes quite blank. Then he said, 'Have you put all this rubbish in a report to Strathbane?'

'Not yet. I haven't any hard proof. But now I know it was you, I'll dig and dig until I get it.'

'It's snowing hard,' said Paul mildly. 'You won't get to Strathbane tonight.'

'I'll get you,' said Hamish, rising to his feet. 'And it won't take me long.'

Elspeth paced up and down in her hotel room. She was bored and restless. Matthew was somewhere with Freda. They should leave in the morning, but the blizzard was so bad that she doubted they would even get out of the car park.

Now that she was supposed to be returning to Glasgow, she wished she could stay in Lochdubh and pick up her old job.

In Glasgow she was just one of many reporters. When she had been working for the *Highland Times*, she had been pretty much her own boss. She realized with a shock that she missed the flower shows, the game fairs and the Highland Games.

There was a knock at the door. Matthew at last, thought Elspeth. He should start to pack just in case the snow stops and the snowploughs can let us get on the road.

'Coming,' she shouted.

She went and unlocked the door. Paul Gibson stood there, his eyes blazing, holding a gun on her.

'Back into the room,' he said. He shut the door behind him. 'Sit down by the phone.'

Elspeth sat down at the desk.

'Now listen to me carefully. Your boyfriend, Hamish Macbeth, is going to file a report saying he thinks I am the murderer. You will phone him now and tell him to drop it or I will shoot you. You will tell him if he tells the police and I see one policeman outside, I will shoot you. Do it now!'

Elspeth phoned the police station. When Hamish answered, she said, 'Hamish, it's me, Elspeth. Paul Gibson's got a gun and he's threatening to shoot me if you send anything about him to Strathbane. He says he'll also shoot me if he sees one policeman outside the hotel.'

'Sit tight,' said Hamish urgently. 'Don't do anything to alarm him. Keep him talking.'

Elspeth rang off. 'You can't keep me here indefinitely,' she said, amazed her voice was steady. 'To use a well-worn phrase, you won't get away with this.'

'Oh, I will. You see, the Lone Ranger will come looking for you. I'll shoot both of you and make it look like a lovers' quarrel.'

Elspeth opened her mouth to tell him he was mad but shut it again. He had gone over the edge. Keep him talking.

'You knew John Heppel before, didn't you?' she asked.

'I wrote to him once. I wanted to dramatize his book. I didn't think much of it, but I thought there was enough there to make a dark drama. I wrote a lot of flattering guff I didn't mean. That's how he remembered me, and he asked Harry Tarrant if I could direct.'

'But why kill him? You could simply have gone to Tarrant and pointed out that the script was unworkable.'

'God, I tried. The silly bugger said, "You don't know literature when you see it. If you can't work with it, I'll find a producer-director who can." It was my big chance. Everyone in Scotland watches *Down in the Glen*. It was scheduled to be shown in England next year. No one was going to get in my way.'

Hamish, what on earth can you do? wondered Elspeth miserably.

Hamish approached the back of the Tommel Castle Hotel on his snowshoes. He let himself in at the kitchen entrance, unstrapped the snowshoes, and propped them against the wall. Clarry, the chef, was enjoying a quiet glass of sherry and stared in surprise at Hamish.

'Clarry,' said Hamish urgently, 'there's a man with a gun in Elspeth's room. Get the manager in here.'

Clarry hurried off and came back shortly with Mr Johnson. 'What's this about a gunman?' asked the manager.

Hamish told him. 'I need to get into Elspeth's room. This castle is full of back passages and things. Any way I can get in there?'

The manager shook his head. 'You'll need to get a squad up from Strathbane.'

'Can't do that. It's Paul Gibson. If he sees so much as a uniform, he'll shoot her. He's got nothing to lose now. He's been fired.'

Upstairs, Elspeth fumbled in her handbag, which was on the desk.

'What are you doing?' demanded Paul.

'Looking for a cigarette.'

'Leave it.'

'Okay.'

But Elspeth had managed to switch on the small tape recorder she carried in her bag, and she left the bag wide open.

'Why mothballs?' she asked. 'What put that idea in your head?'

'Because he was like a sodding great moth, batting against my light whenever I tried to do anything. I'd distilled a solution and held the gun on him till he drank it. Then when he was dying, I got into his computer and wiped out that rotten script. No one was going to complain about my script. They'd all had enough of John except Miss Mimsy, Alice

Patty, burbling on about what a genius her dear John was.'

'So you had to kill her as well?'

'She phoned me up in tears and said that she was sure I had killed John, that John had told her I had threatened his life. I told her to sit tight and I would come round and explain everything. I told her I had proof that Patricia Wheeler had done it. She loved hearing that because she was still jealous of Patricia. I drugged a bottle of wine and took it round.'

I'm going to die, thought Elspeth miserably. I don't think Hamish can get me out of this.

'We could take a tray up and say, "Room service", and put some drugged drink on the tray,' suggested Clary.

'He'd just make her say to leave it outside the door,' said Hamish.

'I could say she had to sign for it, and when she opens the door, we could rush him.'

'He'd shoot her in the back. He's deranged.'

'So how do we smoke him out?' asked Mr Johnson.

Hamish stared at him and then said, 'That's it! You start the fire alarm, get whoever is who has the keys to the television vans in the forecourt, and usher everyone into them so they don't freeze to death. Clarry, we need something that makes really black smoke and those old-fashioned bellows from the lounge fire.'

Paul had fallen silent, although the gun in his hand never wavered. At last he said, 'Where's that boyfriend of yours?'

'He's not my boyfriend,' said Elspeth wearily. 'Didn't it cross your mind he might not bother, that he might just be waiting for reinforcements from Strathbane?'

'Then you're dead.'

Paul jumped as the fire alarm sounded through the hotel. Elspeth half rose. 'Stay where you are,' he shouted.

They began to hear people running along the corridor. Faintly she could hear someone shouting, 'Fire!'

There came a pounding at the door and then Matthew's voice. 'Elspeth, are you in there? The hotel's on fire.'

Then Freda's voice. 'Come on, Matthew. She's probably downstairs.' Then the sound of retreating footsteps.

'It's not on fire,' said Paul. 'It's that copper thinking he can trick me into coming out.'

Keeping the gun trained on Elspeth, Paul went to the window and twitched aside the curtain. Down below, he could see figures hurrying through the blizzard and into the mobile units. Some were turning and pointing up at the building.

'It must be a trick,' he said.

'I don't think so,' said Elspeth. 'Look!'

She pointed at the door.

Acrid black smoke was beginning to seep under it. 'We've got to get out of here,' shouted Elspeth. 'The place really is on fire.'

'Stay where you are! No, open the window.'

Elspeth tried. 'I can't. It's sealed shut.'

'Get to the door and unlock it.' Elspeth did as she was told. 'Now stand back. I'm going to take a look. One move from you and I'll kill you. You'll see it's a trick.'

Paul looked round into the corridor. It was filled with black smoke, and to his horror, he saw red flames leaping up at the end.

'Come on,' he said. 'We're leaving. Get in front of me.' He dug the gun into her back. 'Now move!'

Choking and gasping, they headed for the stairs. All the lights were out.

Suddenly a tall dark figure materialized and Paul's wrist was seized in an iron grip.

'Run, Elspeth!' shouted Hamish.

Paul struggled and fought like the madman he had become. At the top of the stairs Hamish smashed Paul's wrist down on the banister. He let out a cry of pain and dropped the gun, which fell down the stairwell.

Hamish grabbed him by the ankles and held the struggling, screaming director upside down over the stairwell.

Clarry's calm voice sounded in Hamish's ear. 'Just pull him up and handcuff him and caution him, Hamish. There's a good lad. No point in killing him.'

Hamish and Clarry pulled Paul back up. Hamish handcuffed him and cautioned him.

Somehow word had got around about what was really happening. The dishwasher had overheard the plan and had told the under-chef, who had told the maître d', who had told the barman, and so when Paul was led hand-cuffed down the stairs, it was to find television cameras pointed at him, recording his arrest. He let out an unearthly yell and was still screaming when they locked him in the office and Hamish phoned Strathbane and asked for a police helicopter to lift them off.

He found Elspeth at his elbow. 'Are you all right?' he asked. Her face was black with smoke.

'I feel a bit sick. I'll be worse tomorrow when the shock sets in.'

'I should get you to a hospital. You'll be suffering from smoke inhalation.'

'I'm fine. You've got your murderer and I've got a great story.'

'The trouble is,' said Hamish, 'if he ever recovered his wits, he can deny the whole thing. It's going to be one of those cases based on circumstantial evidence. Oh, we can get him for holding you at gunpoint, but if he gets a clever lawyer, the lawyer will try to persuade the jury that because of one crime, the police were fitting him up for another.'

Her silvery eyes gleamed. 'Hamish, I've got him saying he did it on tape.'

'You darling! How? Where?'

'I told him I was looking in my handbag for a cigarette, and I switched on my tape recorder.'

'Could you go and get it? I'd better stay here outside the office just in case he tries to make a break for it.'

Elspeth darted off. Clarry, the chef, had reverted in manner to the days when he used to be on the police force. 'Move along there,' he was saying to the onlookers. 'There's nothing to see. Guests, go back to your rooms, and you television lot go back to the lounge and Mr Johnson will find you rooms for the night.'

Mr Johnson came up to Hamish. 'The snow's stopped, but I'm getting all those mobile units moved out on to the road, or the helicopter won't be able to land.'

'Where's Matthew Campbell?' asked Hamish.

'He was snogging with the schoolteacher in the corner of the bar. Here he comes.'

'Where's Elspeth?' asked Matthew.

'She's probably up in her room filing the story of a lifetime. Didn't you hear what was going on? She was held by the murderer at gunpoint.'

Freda came up and put her arm through Matthew's. 'What's going on?'

'Come with me,' said Matthew. 'I've been missing out on a great story.'

Hamish waited and fidgeted. What was taking Elspeth so long?

At last she appeared and handed him the tape. 'It's all there.'

'What kept you?'

'I was making a copy. He's very quiet in there. Is he all right?'

Hamish unlocked the office door. Paul was sitting slumped in a chair, his handcuffed hands behind him. His eyes were vacant. Hamish locked the door again.

'I think he's lost it,' he said. 'I think this is one that won't stand trial. His lawyer will claim he's unfit to stand because of insanity.'

'I'd better get back upstairs,' said Elspeth. 'I'm going to have heavy expenses. My suitcase was open on the bed with my clothes in it, and they're all soot-blackened. What did you use for the fire?'

'Clarry scorched a mixture of rubber and something on a stove, and we lit a fire in a steel bin at the end of the corridor. Are you sure you shouldn't be going to hospital?'

'No, I'm fine. Got to go.'

Then Hamish heard the roar of a helicopter and went to the door of the hotel. The snow had stopped, but the blades of the helicopter were whipping up a blizzard of their own.

Jimmy Anderson and his colleague, Harry MacNab, were the first out, followed by policemen.

'He's in the office, Jimmy,' said Hamish, 'and here's a tape of his confession. But he seems to have lost his wits, so I don't think you'll get much out of him.'

'Faking it?'

'I don't think so. I think he was insane all along and now he's gone over the edge.'

'You've solved this case. You'd better come back to Strathbane with us.'

'Would you mind handling it yourself, Jimmy? I've left my dog at the police station.'

'For heaven's sake, Hamish.'

'I'll send over a full report. Honest.'

'What exactly happened?'

In a few brief sentences Hamish outlined how he had begun to suspect Paul, about the kidnapping of Elspeth and the rescue.

'Right. I'll take him in. Don't you want to come back with us and rub Blair's nose in it?'

'No, I'm fine. You go ahead.'

'He'll try to take the credit.'

'Let him.'

'Hamish, you could get that friend of yours, Angela, to look after Lugs. You don't want Daviot to hear how you solved the case in case he promotes you out of Lochdubh.'

'Maybe.'

'I think there's more than one madman here.

260

Anyway, get that statement over as soon as possible.'

'Where is Blair, by the way?'

'He'd checked out for the night. I'll wake him up when we get back.'

Hamish retrieved his snowshoes from the kitchen and strapped them on outside. But when he reached the road, he was able to take them off again. The road had been ploughed and gritted again. The cities of the south might wait in vain for a snowplough or gritter, but the little roads of Sutherland were well serviced. He trudged down to the police station.

When he switched on the kitchen light, nothing happened. He fished out an old hurricane lamp and lit it. Lugs woke up and demanded food. Hamish gave him a dog biscuit instead. Lugs was getting too fat and had been fed already.

He felt bone-weary, but he knew that with a power cut, his computer wouldn't work and he would have to go to Strathbane, after all.

Chapter Thirteen

In my time, the follies of the town crept slowly among us, but now they travel faster than a stagecoach.
— Oliver Goldsmith

Hamish peered up at the blazing stars as he drove along. The winds of Sutherland were like stage curtains, whipping back the clouds to reveal another scene. A small pale blue moon cast an eerie light over the white landscape.

When he crested a rise and saw Strathbane below him, it had been sanitized by snow, lights twinkling through the whiteness like a Christmas card. His parents had told him that Strathbane had once been a prosperous fishing port but that a combination of highland laziness and brutal European Union fishing quotas had sent it into decline. Then a new motorway from the south had been built, allowing drugs and villains to travel north in comfort and set up new markets.

He parked outside police headquarters and went up to the detectives' room. Jimmy hailed him. 'They're keeping him under suicide watch for the night until the police psychiatrist interviews him in the morning. Why did you decide to come?'

Hamish told him about the power cut. 'Well, grab a computer and start typing,' said Jimmy.

As he typed his report, Hamish could only marvel that his obsession with that script had paid off. He had once been on a case where a scriptwriter had been murdered by an author. What made some writers and would-be writers so dangerously vain and unstable? Maybe they were like actors, always craving attention, not quite grown up.

Hamish just wanted to get the report finished and get home. It was a relief to think that Superintendent Daviot would be safely home in bed, and by the time he turned up for work in the morning, Blair would be ready and waiting to take the credit.

He did not know that at that very moment Blair was closeted upstairs in the super's office, talking to Daviot.

'This is good work,' Daviot was saying, 'and it was right of you to wake me up.'

Blair thought quickly. It would be a tortuous business trying to hide the fact that it was Macbeth who had solved the two murders. But on the other hand, if Macbeth got the kudos, Daviot would once more want him transferred to Strathbane. Before Macbeth could be promoted, there would be assessments and exams. Macbeth would hate that. And with any luck, while it was all going on, the police station at Lochdubh would be closed down.

'As a matter of fact,' said Blair with the oily smile he always had on his face when talking to his superior, 'it was Macbeth that solved the whole thing.'

He outlined how Hamish had found the original script and had leapt to the conclusion that the murderer was Paul Gibson, about Elspeth being held hostage, and about her rescue.

'So I was thinking, sir, that Macbeth is wasted up in that village. We could do with him here.'

Daviot studied Blair's face. He knew that Blair loathed Hamish and that his suggestion was prompted by spite. But Blair was the type of officer that Daviot felt comfortable with. He was always polite and a good member of the Freemasons. One always knew where one was with men like Blair, whereas the maverick Macbeth was another thing entirely.

'Where is Macbeth?' he asked.

Daviot's secretary, Helen, came in at that moment with a tray of coffee. Women's liberation had passed Daviot by, and he had summoned Helen to headquarters and when she arrived ordered her to make coffee.

'I believe Hamish Macbeth is in the detect-ives' room, sir.'

'Good, good. Send him up. I'll have a word in private with him.'

Hamish had just finished his report when he got the summons to go upstairs. His heart was in his boots. Blair had just come in and shouted, 'Grand work, Macbeth. I told the super how well you'd done.'

Daviot surveyed Hamish when he entered. Hamish needed a shave, red bristles were showing on his chin, his shirt was dirty at the collar, and he smelled of burning rubber.

'Sit down, Hamish,' said Daviot. 'Helen, a cup of coffee for the officer.'

Helen, who disliked Hamish, slammed a cup of coffee down in front of him so that some of the liquid spilled into the saucer.

When Helen had left, Daviot said, 'You have done very well.'

'Thank you, sir.'

'Mr Blair agrees with me that talents such as yours are wasted in a highland village.'

'With all respect, sir, I was able to solve these murders because I was able to use my own initiative. If I were in Strathbane, I would just be another policeman and would have to take orders. I might have to spend a lot of my time on traffic duty.' And Blair would see to that, thought Hamish gloomily.

Daviot leaned forward. 'But if you were to become a detective, that would be another matter.'

'If I left Lochdubh and you closed down the police station, that would leave Cnothan and Lochdubh without a police officer. Who would then check on the frail and elderly in the out-lying crofts?'

'I am sure that could all be done from here.'

'I don't think the press would like it either,' pursued Hamish. 'The first time an old lady up on the moors has a fall in her croft house and is left lying there for twenty-four hours, the papers would take you to the cleaners . . . sir.'

Daviot frowned. He knew Hamish had friends in the press, not to mention that girl-friend of his who worked for the *Bugle*.

'And,' went on Hamish eagerly, 'do you know of anyone in Strathbane who ever wants to go north of here even on their days off? They go down to Inverness or Perth.'

'Detective Chief Inspector Heather Meikle is anxious to get you transferred to Inverness.'

'Sir, if that were to happen, I would end up suing the chief inspector for sexual harassment.'

'Well, let's leave that alone for the moment,' said Daviot quickly. He knew of Heather's man-eating reputation. 'There is going to be a great deal of press coverage over this.'

'I'm not good at that at all,' said Hamish. 'The press always likes a senior officer to brief them.'

Daviot visibly brightened. He loved being on television.

Helen put her head round the door. 'Sir, the press are in the front hall and demanding a statement. Mr Blair suggested that PC Macbeth might like to address them.'

'No, no, I'll deal with them myself.'

'With your permission, sir,' said Hamish, 'I'd really like to get home. It's been a long, hard day.'

'Very well, Hamish. Off you go.'

Hamish made his way quietly out of police headquarters by the back door and walked round to the car park. He could see that the front hall of the building was already bright with television lights.

He got in and drove off. He felt relief flooding him as he headed up on to the moors. At one point he braked hard as a deer skittered across the road in front of him and leapt off into the snow.

Then outside Lochdubh, he pulled into a lay-by on the single-track road to let a procession of television vans pass him.

'Go on,' he muttered. 'Get the hell out of my village.'

As he descended into the village, he saw that

the street lights were still out. He searched for his keys outside the police station and found he had forgotten them. He tried the handle of the kitchen door and found he had forgotten to lock it. And to think I give lectures on home security, he thought.

He lit the hurricane lamp again and then the wood stove. He realized he was ravenously hungry and could not remember when he had last eaten. Probably that dinner with Kirsty for which he still had to pay. He got two lamb chops out of the fridge, put a frying pan on the stove, and waited for the chops to cook. Lugs sat up and begged, but Hamish gave him another dog biscuit and told him for the hundredth time that he was on a diet.

The stove had a back boiler, so he knew there would be enough hot water for a shower by the time he finished his meal.

He ate, the kitchen grew warm, the hurricane lamp threw a soft light, and he was beginning to feel drowsy when he heard a wail from outside. Lugs barked and his coat stood on end.

'Good boy. Wait there,' said Hamish.

He opened the kitchen door and looked out. A large cat lay on its side in the snow. It let out a wail again.

Hamish went back in and got the hurricane lamp, tying the bristling, barking Lugs to the table leg.

269

He bent down over the cat. He discovered it had a broken leg. He was sure it was a wild cat with its big head and wide face and yellow eyes now full of pain.

'Will this damn night never end?' he groaned.

He went in and got a blanket and lifted the cat on to it. Its body was lighter than it should be. He thought the animal, unable to hunt, was probably starved. He wondered just how long the leg had been broken.

Shutting the police station, he made his way along to Dr Brodie's and banged on the door.

He waited shivering because he had forgotten to put on his coat. The door finally opened and Angela stood there holding a candle. 'What on earth . . .?'

'It is this damn cat,' said Hamish. 'It is injured.' And then to Angela's horror, he burst into tears.

'Hamish, come in. What's up?'

Hamish wiped his eyes with his sleeve. 'It has been the stressful day, Angela. I caught the murderer and I'm so tired, but I found this cat outside my door and wondered if the doctor could do anything for it.'

Dr Brodie appeared at the foot of the stairs wrapped in his dressing gown and listened impatiently while Angela outlined Hamish's predicament.

'I'm not a vet, Hamish, and that looks like a wild cat. Oh, for God's sake, don't look at me like that. I'll see what I can do. Bring the beast through to the surgery. I'll need to give it a shot of tranquillizer. Angela, start the generator so we get some light. We didn't bother with it because we were going to bed.'

Hamish carried the cat through to the surgery. 'That's right. Lay it on the table there. Angela, Hamish looks a wreck. Take him through and give him a stiff drink.'

Angela led Hamish through to the cluttered living room and went off and started the generator. Then she came back to the living room and raked the dead ashes out of the fire, put on paper and kindling and logs, and struck a match. She went into the kitchen and came back with a cup of kerosene and threw the contents on the fire. It exploded into flames with a roar. 'I never could be bothered waiting for the things to light,' she said. She poured Hamish a stiff brandy. 'Get that down you. I know it's not the thing to give people in shock, but I think you're exhausted and need a bracer.'

'I don't know what came over me. I've never cried before.'

'Tell me what happened.'

So Hamish told her the story, ending up by saying, 'I thought I'd lost Elspeth.'

'Maybe you should marry her, Hamish.'

'She's changed. She's all citified. She'd never fit in here now.'

'You won't know until you ask her.'

'Maybe.'

Dr Brodie came in. 'I put a splint on the beast. I'll take it to the vet in the morning, and he'll put it in plaster. Why didn't you wake him?'

'Because both you and Angela love cats,' said Hamish.

'And what are you going to do with this one when it's recovered? A wild cat will never make a house pet. And it would probably kill Lugs.'

'If the vet can mend it, I'll take it up on the moors and get rid of it. Now I'm going home.'

Wearily Hamish showered and put on his pyjamas. He climbed into bed, and Lugs climbed in after him and stretched out at his feet.

He plunged down into vivid dreams of fire and smoke and murder.

In the morning Hamish called headquarters and said he was taking the whole weekend off unless there was any major crime he had to cover. The snow was sparkling under a pale sun as he walked Lugs along the waterfront. He called on Angela and was told that Dr Brodie was at the vet's with the cat. Hamish made his way there.

The vet, Hugh Liddesdale, was not pleased

to see him. 'Brodie's just left. A wild cat, Hamish! A *Felis silvestris grampus*!'

'Can I see it?'

'Come along.' Hugh, a small fussy man who thought all cats were an indulgence and only favoured working animals like sheepdogs, led him through to a line of cages. The wild cat was sleeping.

'I got it to take some food. It's a splendid beast, I'll grant you that.'

'Are there any pure wild cats left in the Highlands?'

'I think they've all been mongrelized over the centuries. But this one's still a big creature.'

The cat was larger than a household one, with a big proud head, tabby markings and a bushy tail with two black rings at the tip.

'Do you think it'll make it?'

'The break was clean and recent.'

'How did it get starved, then?'

'Well, it's a mystery for you to solve. The only thing I can think of is that someone caught this and kept it and ill-treated it. I wouldn't advise you to keep it.'

'No, I wouldn't do that to Lugs. When it's healed, I'll let it loose on the moors.'

'This is going to cost you, Hamish.'

Hamish sighed, thinking of the dinner bill at the Tommel Castle Hotel.

Hugh threw him a sympathetic look. 'I tell you what. When you get my bill, just pay it off weekly.'

'Thanks, Hugh.'

'Of course, a nice wild salmon would defray the cost.' Everyone in Lochdubh knew that Hamish occasionally poached salmon.

'I'll see what I can do.'

Lugs sat silently at Hamish's feet, staring curiously at the cat. Hamish was amazed that the dog neither bristled nor barked.

'Aye, well, I'll leave you to it,' said the vet.

Hamish went back to the police station but found he could not enjoy the peace and quiet. The thought of that computer up in the loft was haunting him. The telephone rang. He reluctantly answered it.

It was Elspeth. 'Hamish, I'm leaving this afternoon. We should talk.'

'Come here in an hour's time,' said Hamish.

He climbed up to the loft and collected the computer. 'It's a cold day, Lugs, but we're going for a row in a boat.' Lugs wagged his tail almost as if he knew what Hamish was saying. Lugs loved going out on the loch.

Hamish put the computer in a plastic shopping bag and walked along to the pub with Lugs. He found Archie Maclean propping up the bar. The little fisherman was dressed in his usual tight clothes. His wife was a fanatical housekeeper and boiled all the clothes in a copper so that everything that Archie wore had shrunk.

'Can I take your rowboat out, Archie?'

'It's a right cold day, Hamish. Won't be much good for the fishing.'

'I feel like getting a bit of exercise and there's nothing like a good row.'

'Help yourself. You know where it is.'

Hamish went down to the beach to where the boat was tied up at the foot of stone steps leading down from the harbour. He lifted Lugs in, settled himself, and picked up the oars.

He rowed and rowed to the middle of the loch, feeling all the tension leaving his body. He would talk to Elspeth and see what they could work out.

When he judged he was far enough out, he slipped the bag with the computer over the side and watched it spiral down into the icy waters of the sea loch.

Then he glanced at his watch. He had better row back fast or he would miss Elspeth.

He was just nearing the shore when he saw, to his horror, Heather Meikle standing outside the police station clutching a bottle. He rowed quickly round the far side of the harbour until he was out of sight.

'What are you doing here?' Elspeth asked Heather.

'I'm waiting for Hamish. We have a lot to talk about. Where is he?'

'He may have been called to Strathbane.'

'His Land Rover's still here. I'll wait.'

'I have an appointment with him,' said Elspeth.

Heather glared. 'Well, as his superior officer, I think my visit comes first.'

Matthew drove up and honked the horn. 'Are you coming, Elspeth? We'd better get on the road.'

Elspeth gave a little shrug and joined Matthew in the car.

'No sign of lover boy?' asked Matthew.

'Shut up and drive. You've got my case in the back, haven't you?'

'Yes.'

They drove a little way in silence. Elspeth twisted her head and watched Lochdubh disappearing behind her.

'You know, Matthew,' she said, 'I've been thinking of asking Sam for my old job back.'

'God, you should have told me!'

'Why?'

'Freda and I are going to be married, and I asked Sam for a job and he's given me one.'

'Matthew. He can't take on both of us.'

'Look at it this way: I'm getting married and you aren't.'

'No, I'm not,' said Elspeth in a small sad voice.

Hamish finally tied the rowboat up at other steps on the far side of the harbour. He carried Lugs up and made his way to the pub. Archie was sitting at a table in the corner, playing dominoes.

'Archie, another favour,' said Hamish. 'Detective Chief Inspector Heather Meikle is outside the police station. She might be waiting in her car. Could you tell her I've gone off to Inverness clubbing with Freda? And your boat's at the foot of the steps on the far side of the harbour. I didn't want her to see me.'

'All right, Hamish. Back in a tick.'

Archie made his way to the police station. He went to a car that was parked in front of it and peered into the driver's side. Heather Meikle had a bottle of whisky and a glass and was just helping herself to another drink. 'What is it?' she snapped. 'What do you want?'

'Hamish Macbeth has gone off to Inverness to go clubbing with our schoolteacher.'

'Rats!'

Heather drained her glass in one long gulp. She screwed the top on to the bottle and put glass and bottle on the floor. Archie drew back as she drove off.

Then he returned to report to Hamish.

'I hope that's the last I'll see of her,' said Hamish. He went to the police station, and although it was only late afternoon, he fell on the bed with his clothes on and plunged back down into sleep.

Just before he had gone to sleep, he vowed to ring Elspeth on her mobile and explain what had happened.

But he did not awake until six o'clock the following morning.

Jimmy Anderson phoned him later in the morning. 'Was our Heather over at Lochdubh to see you yesterday?'

'Aye. But I kept out o' sight.'

'She had a crash.'

'Oh, God. Where?'

'On the Lochdubh–Strathbane road. She found the only tree by the road and crashed right into it. She was as drunk as a skunk.'

'Is she seriously hurt?'

'Not a scratch. But her alcohol intake was so great they pumped her out, and they're keeping her in Strathbane Hospital for observation.'

'I should maybe have seen her, but, man, I was frightened that that one would eat me alive. Is Paul Gibson fit to be interviewed?'

'No. The psychiatrist says his mind's gone. We've been ferreting into his background. Seems he once worked on a police series, and they had a man there showing the actors how to break in to a car. That must have been how he learned to hot-wire that van. What are you doing now?'

'I'm still off duty, and I plan to eat and sleep.'

Hamish phoned Elspeth on her mobile. It was switched off. He tried her flat in Glasgow and got an answering service. He did not want to leave a message. He would try her later.

He took himself and Lugs along to the Italian restaurant, and he ate a large meal while the waiter, Willie Lamont, led Lugs off to the kitchen to spoil the dog with a large helping of osso bucco.

When he returned to the police station, he checked his messages. There was one from Elspeth. 'It was typical of you not to turn up,' she said. 'Face up to it. You don't want to marry me. In fact, I don't think you want to marry anyone.'

Hamish felt guilty and ashamed because deep down he felt a little surge of relief.

Epilogue

A week after the arrest of Paul Gibson, the vet phoned Hamish. 'Come and get your cat. It's spooking the other animals.'

'Is the plaster off?'

'Of course not. But you'll need to look after it yourself.'

Hamish decided to take Lugs with him. If the dog saw him taking the cat home, he might not react so badly.

'Can it walk?' he asked Hugh.

'Yes, it can limp around with the plaster on. But you'd better keep her indoors.'

'It's a she-cat?'

'Yes. What are you going to call it?'

'Nothing at all, since I'm going to let her free as soon as the plaster's off. How long exactly?'

'Bring her back in three weeks' time.'

'Three weeks!'

The vet put on a pair of thick gloves before lifting the cat out of the cage. He handed her to Hamish.

Hamish expected her to twist and fight, but she lay supine in his arms.

'She's still weak,' said the vet. 'But look out when she recovers her energy.'

Hamish carried the cat back to the police station. Lugs plodded amiably beside him.

'What's up with you, Lugs?' demanded Hamish. 'I thought you'd be barking your head off.'

At the police station he found two mackerel laid out on a plate on the table with a note from Angela: 'For your cat.' The news that Hugh had ordered him to take the cat home must have already gone round the village. Angela had obviously let herself in with the new spare key that Hamish had put in the gutter. Now the computer was gone, he didn't see any reason to keep visitors locked out.

Hamish put the cat on the floor. He put one of the fish on a plate and set it down beside her.

The cat ate ravenously while Lugs calmly watched. 'I don't understand you,' said Hamish to his dog. 'Another animal eating, a cat at that, and you don't bother! I just can't make it out.'

Hamish put Lugs on the leash and went along to Patel's and bought cat litter and a litter tray. When he returned, there was no sign of the cat. He wondered whether she had slipped out after him.

But when he went into his bedroom, the cat was lying asleep, stretched out with her head on the pillow.

Hamish phoned Angela. 'Thanks for the fish. I was wondering . . .'

'No, Hamish. I love my cats, and that beast would eat them.'

'It's awfy quiet. Just like a house cat.'

'It's still recovering. No, Hamish. It's all yours.'

The snow had melted and a soft wind was blowing up the sea loch from the Atlantic when Hamish went to the vet and watched as the plaster was taken off.

'She'll limp a bit,' said Hugh, 'but she should soon get the full strength back in that leg. I'm surprised to see you and Lugs in one piece.'

'I'm surprised, too, Hugh. She's right quiet.'

'Take my advice and get rid of the thing as soon as possible.' The cat stared at Hamish.

'She iss not a thing,' protested Hamish. 'She iss one fine animal.'

'Don't be daft and get any ideas of keeping her. She belongs in the wild.'

Hamish carried the cat back to the police station despite Hugh's protests that he ought to be carrying such a dangerous animal in a cat box. He let the cat out in the kitchen and said to Lugs, 'It's the grand day. We'll just go for a stroll.'

He opened the kitchen door. Lugs went out and the cat slid after him.

'No, you don't,' said Hamish. 'Get back in.' He bent down to lift the cat but she moved away from him. He looked at her curiously, then he began to walk away with Lugs at his heels. The cat followed behind Lugs, and the odd procession made its way along the waterfront.

Mrs Wellington hailed him. 'You shouldn't be letting that animal on the loose.'

Hamish stopped. Lugs sat down and waited and the cat sat beside him.

'Doesn't look dangerous to me,' said Hamish. 'Leave the beast alone.'

But he knew the day was approaching when he would need to turn the cat loose.

In late spring Hamish put the cat in the Land Rover in the back and lifted Lugs on to the passenger seat and drove up high on the moors.

The air was full of the smell of growing things, and there was a tang of salt in the air.

He stopped the Land Rover and lifted Lugs down, then got the cat out of the back and set her down in the heather.

'Go now,' said Hamish. 'You're free!'

The cat sat and stared at him.

With a little sigh Hamish lifted Lugs back in and got into the Land Rover himself and drove off, glancing in the rear-view mirror until the cat was no longer in sight.

'It's you and me again,' he said to Lugs inside the police station, trying not to admit to himself that he missed the cat already. He had thought Lugs would have put up some sort of protest because the dog and cat had become inseparable.

He went off on his rounds for the rest of the day, resisting the temptation to go back where he had left the cat to see if she was all right.

When he returned, he cooked dinner for himself and Lugs and went into the office to do some paperwork.

Lugs gave one sharp peremptory bark. Hamish went into the kitchen. The dog was staring at the kitchen door and wagging his tail.

Hamish opened the door. The cat trudged wearily in. She went straight to the bedroom and leapt up on the bed and fell asleep.

'Well, I'll be damned,' said Hamish Macbeth.

* * *

By autumn that year Alistair Taggart's short novel, *Home of the Eagles*, was published. The first half of the book was in Gaelic and the second half was the English translation. It was nominated for the Booker Prize. It sold very well in the south, where people displayed it on their coffee tables and didn't read it. Angela was still working on her novel.

Freda and Matthew were married by Mr Wellington. Elspeth arrived for the ceremony. Hamish felt a desperate need to talk to her, accompanied by a desperate need to keep out of her way.

He had just made up his mind late on into the reception to take her aside and talk to her when he found out she had left for Glasgow. He knew he had holidays owing. He could always go down to Glasgow and see her.

But as winter began to clamp its icy fingers round the Highlands again, as the purple heather faded to dull brown, Hamish was still in Lochdubh with his odd cat, now called Sonsie, christened by Archie Maclean, who said the cat's broad face brought to mind Burns's 'To a Haggis': 'Fair fa' your honest sonsie face.'

One clear cold evening he went out on to the waterfront. Life had become blissfully quiet. He felt there was really nothing to stop him going to Glasgow except his pets. Many would be happy to look after Lugs, but none wanted the cat.

Then he saw Priscilla Halburton-Smythe, his ex-fiancée, walking towards him. At first he thought he was imagining things, but she came up to him and they both leaned on the sea wall and looked out on the black waters of the loch.

'You've been having a lot of adventures since I was last here,' said Priscilla.

'It's lovely and quiet now.' The moon shone down on the diamond engagement ring on Priscilla's finger. There was no wedding ring.

'Not married yet?' said Hamish.

'No.'

'Me neither.'

They both leaned together on the sea wall in silence. There seemed to be so much to say on the one hand, and on the other, no need to say anything at all.

If you enjoyed *Death of a Bore*, read on for the first chapter of the next book in the *Hamish Macbeth* series . . .

DEATH OF A DREAMER

Chapter One

So, if I dream I have you, I have you,
For, all our joys are but fantastical.
                                        – John Donne

It had been a particularly savage winter in the county of Sutherland at the very north of Scotland. Great blizzards had roared in off the Atlantic, burying roads and cottages in deep snowdrifts. Patel's, the local grocery shop in the village of Lochdubh, sold out of nearly everything, and at one point it was necessary for rescue helicopters to drop supplies to the beleaguered inhabitants.

And then, at the end of March, the last of the storms roared away, to be followed by balmy breezes and blue skies. The air was full of the sound of rasping saws and the thump of hammers as the inhabitants of Lochdubh, as if they had awakened from a long sleep, got to work repairing storm damage.

The police station was comparatively sheltered below the brow of a hill and had escaped the worst of the ravages of winter. Police Constable Hamish Macbeth found that the only thing in need of repair was the roof of the hen house.

Archie Macleod, one of the local fishermen, went to call on Hamish and found the lanky policeman with the flaming red hair up on top of a ladder, busily hammering nails into the roof of the hen house.

'Fine day, Hamish,' he called.

Glad of any diversion from work, Hamish climbed down the ladder. 'I was just about to put the kettle on, Archie. Fancy a cup of tea?'

'Aye, that would be grand.'

Archie followed Hamish into the kitchen and sat at the table while Hamish put an old blackened kettle on the woodburning stove.

'Got much damage, Archie?'

'Tiles off the roof. But herself is up there doing the repairs.'

Hamish's hazel eyes glinted with amusement. 'Didn't feel like helping her, did you?'

'Och, no. The womenfolk are best left on their own. How have you been doing?'

'Very quiet. There's one thing about a bad winter,' said Hamish over his shoulder as he took a pair of mugs down from a cupboard. 'It stops the villains driving up from the south to look for easy pickings in the cottages.'

'Aye, and it keeps folks sweet as well. Nothing like the blitz spirit. How did that newcomer survive the winter, or did herself take off for the south?'

The newcomer was Effie Garrard. Hamish had called on her last summer when she first arrived, and had been sure she would not stay long. He put her down as one of those romantic dreamers who sometimes relocate to the Highlands, looking for what they always describe as 'the quality of life'.

'I sent gamekeeper Henry up to see her last month, and he said the place was all shut up.'

The kettle started to boil. As he filled the teapot, Hamish thought uneasily about Effie. He should really have called on her himself. What if the poor woman had been lying there dead inside when Henry called?

'Tell you what, Archie. I'll take a run up there and chust see if the woman's all right.' The sudden sibilance of Hamish's highland accent betrayed that he was feeling guilty.

That afternoon, Hamish got into the police Land Rover, fighting off the attempts of his dog, Lugs, and his cat, Sonsie, to get into it as well. 'I'll take you two out for a walk later,' he called.

He saw the Currie sisters, Nessie and Jessie, standing on the road watching him. The car windows were down, and he clearly heard Nessie say, 'That man's gone dotty. Talking to the beasts as if they were the humans.'

293

Hamish flushed angrily as he drove off. His adoption of the cat, a wild cat, had caused a lot of comment in the village, people complaining that it was impossible to domesticate such an animal. But Sonsie appeared to have settled down and had showed no signs of leaving.

Effie Garrard had bought a small one-storey cottage up in the hills above Lochdubh. It had a roof of corrugated iron, stone floors, and a fireplace that smoked. When Hamish had first visited her, he found her to be a small woman in her forties, sturdy, with brown hair speckled with grey, a round red-cheeked face, and a small pursed mouth. She had gushed on about the majesty of the Highlands and how she planned to sell her 'art works' in the local shops.

If she were still alive, and he hoped to God she was, he expected to find that she had packed up and gone, all her fantasies of a highland life shattered.

But as he approached her cottage, he saw smoke rising up from the chimney. Maybe she had sold it to someone else, he thought, and because of the rigours of the winter which had kept most people indoors, he hadn't heard about it.

But it was Effie herself who answered the door to him. 'You should really get the phone put in,' said Hamish. 'Something could have happened to you during the winter, and we'd never have known if you needed help.'

'I've got a mobile.'

'Does it work up here? There still seem to be blank spots all over the Highlands.'

'Yes, it works fine. Are you coming in for tea?'

'Thanks.' Hamish removed his cap and ducked his head to get through the low doorway.

The living room and kitchen combined had a long work table with a pottery wheel on it. On the table were a few vases and bowls glazed in beautiful colours.

'Yours?' asked Hamish, picking up a little bowl of sapphire blue and turning it around in his fingers.

'Yes. Mr Patel has taken some, and the gift shop at the Tommel Castle Hotel has taken a good few more. I didn't do any business during the winter because of the bad weather, but I'm hoping for sales when the visitors come back.'

There were paintings of birds and flowers hanging on the walls, each one an exquisite little gem. Hamish was beginning to revise his opinion of Effie. She was a talented artist.

'I'm surprised you survived the winter up here,' he said.

'I didn't have to. Coffee or tea?'

'Coffee would be grand. Just black. What do you mean, you didn't have to?'

'I went to stay with my sister in Brighton, and so I escaped the worst of it. Do sit down and don't loom over me.'

295

Hamish sat down on a hard chair at a corner of the work table while she prepared coffee. 'Odd,' he said. 'I thought the Highlands would have driven you out by now.'

'Why? This is the most beautiful place in the world.'

Yes, thought Hamish cynically, if you can afford to get out of the place for the winter.

Aloud, he said, 'Oh, I put you down as one of those romantics.'

'There is nothing wrong with being romantic. Everyone needs dreams. Here's your coffee.

Hamish looked at the little blue bowl. 'That bowl. Is it for sale?'

'Of course.'

'How much?'

'Fifty pounds.'

'Fifty pounds!' Hamish stared at her.

'It's a work of art,' she said calmly. 'Fifty pounds is cheap at the price.'

A hard businesswoman as well, thought Hamish. Still, it meant he had been wrong about her. Romantically minded newcomers had caused trouble in the past.

In April there was one last blizzard – the lambing blizzard, as the locals called it – and then the fine weather returned, and by June, one long sunny day followed another. Memories of the black winter receded. It stayed light even in the middle of the night. Amazingly, for

296

Hamish, there was still no crime, not even petty theft.

He was strolling along the waterfront one fine morning when he was stopped by a tall man with an easel strapped on his back who said he was looking for accommodation.

'I don't think there's a place here with a studio available,' said Hamish.

The man laughed. 'I'm a landscape painter. I work outside.' He thrust out a hand. 'I'm Jock Fleming.'

'Hamish Macbeth. You could try Mrs Dunne along at Sea View, just along the end there. You can't miss it.'

Jock looked down at the dog and the cat, waiting patiently at Hamish's heels. 'That's an odd pair of animals you've got there,' he said.

'They're company,' said Hamish dismissively.

'Really? It's a good thing I'm not superstitious, or I'd be crossing myself,' said Jock with an easy laugh. 'A wild cat and a dog with blue eyes!'

Hamish grinned. He took an instant liking to the artist. He was a powerful man in, Hamish judged, his early forties with shaggy black hair streaked with grey. He had a comical, battered-looking face and seemed to find himself a bit of a joke.

'When you've got settled in,' said Hamish, 'drop by the police station and we'll have a dram.'

'Great. See you.'

Hamish watched him go. 'Well, Lugs,' he said. 'That'll be one incomer who won't be any trouble at all.'

Hamish was disappointed as two days passed and Jock did not call for that drink. But on the third day, as he walked along the waterfront in the morning, he saw Jock at his easel, surrounded by a little group of women.

Walking up to the group, Hamish said, 'Move along, ladies The man can't do any work with you bothering him.'

'I don't mind,' said Jock cheerfully. 'I like the company of beautiful ladies.'

Freda, the schoolteacher, giggled and said, 'He's giving us lessons. Why don't you run along, Hamish?'

'Yes,' agreed Nessie Currie. 'Go and catch a criminal or something.'

'I'll see you later for that dram, Hamish,' called Jock as Hamish walked off.

I hope that one isn't going to turn out to be a heartbreaker, thought Hamish. He decided to visit Angela Brodie, the doctor's wife.

The kitchen door was open, so he walked straight in. Angela was sitting at the kitchen table at her computer. She looked up when she saw Hamish and gave a sigh of relief, pushing a wisp of hair out of her eyes.

'I can't get on with this book, Hamish,' she complained. 'When the first one was published, I thought I was all set. But the words won't come.'

'Maybe you're trying too hard.'

'Maybe. Let's have coffee.'

Angela's first novel had been published the previous autumn. Reviews were good, but sales were modest.

'The trouble is I am damned as a "literary writer",' said Angela, 'which usually means praise and no money.'

'Perhaps something in the village will spark your imagination,' said Hamish, covertly shooing two of her cats off the table where they were trying to drink the milk out of the jug.

'Like what?'

'Like this artist fellow. Seems to be a big hit with the ladies.'

'Oh, he jokes and teases them. But I can't see anyone falling for him.'

'Why?'

'In a funny kind of way, there's nothing about him that gives any of them the come-on. He's just a thoroughly nice man.'

'Painting any good?'

'He's just started, but I looked his name up on the Internet. He's considered to be a very good landscape painter. He paints pictures in the old-fashioned way, and people are going for that. I think they're moving away from elephant dung and unmade beds or whatever the modern artist has been exhibiting at the

Tate. I don't think he's going to cause any dramas. Where are your animals?'

'I left them playing in the garden.'

'Don't you find it odd that a dog and a wild cat should get on so well?'

'Not really. A relief, if you ask me. If Lugs hadn't taken to the cat, I'd need to have got rid of it.'

'Be careful, Hamish. It is a wild cat, and they can be savage.'

'I don't think there's such a thing as a pure wild cat any more. They've been interbreeding with the domestic ones for years. When I found Sonsie outside the police station with a broken leg, I didn't think the beast would live. Someone had been mistreating that animal. I'd dearly like to find out who it was.'

'Maybe it just got caught in a trap.'

'I've a feeling Sonsie had been kept captive somewhere.'

'Here's your coffee. Is Effie Garrard still around?'

'Yes. I visited her the other day and asked around about her. Patel is selling her stuff, and so is the gift shop up at the Tommel Castle Hotel. She does charge awfy high prices.'

'Are you going to the ceilidh on Saturday?'

'I might drop in.'

'You'll need a ticket. Five pounds.'

'Five pounds! What on earth for?'

'The church hall needs repainting.'

'I thought some of the locals would have done that for free.'

'Oh, they are. But it's to raise money for repairs to the roof, paint and new curtains.'

'And what would I be getting for five pounds?'

'A buffet supper. The Italian restaurant is doing the catering.'

'That's decent of them. I'll go.'

'You must be getting very bored,' said Angela. 'No crime.'

'And that just suits me fine. No crime now and no crime on the horizon.'

Effie Garrard was a fantasist. Dreams were as essential to her as breathing. While Hamish sat in the doctor's wife's kitchen drinking coffee, Effie approached the village of Lochdubh, wrapped in a dream of attending her own funeral. Villagers wept, the piper played a lament, famous artists came from all over to give their eulogies. She had decided to walk instead of taking her car because the day was so fine. The twin mountains behind the village soared up to a clear blue sky. Little glassy waves on the sea loch made a pleasant plashing sound as they curled on to the shingly beach.

A pleasurable tear ran down Effie's cheek, and she was wondering just how long she could stretch out this splendid dream when she saw Jock at his easel.

Her dream bubble burst as she experienced a jealous pang. She wanted to be the only artist in Lochdubh. Probably some amateur, she thought, approaching him. Jock's coterie of admiring women had left for dinner – dinner in Lochdubh still being in the middle of the day, except in posh places like the Tommel Castle Hotel.

Effie stood behind him and studied his work. His colours were magnificent. He had caught the purplish green of the forestry trees on the other side of the loch, and the reflections in the glassy loch had been painted by the hand of a master.

She did not want to interrupt him, but he turned round and smiled at her. 'Grand day,' said Jock.

'Oh, please go on. I'm an artist myself, and I hate to be interrupted,' said Effie.

'I don't mind. I was just about to take a break. What do you do?'

'Small pictures of birds and flowers, and I'm a potter as well.' She held out her hand. 'Effie Garrard.'

'I'm Jock Fleming. Wait a bit. I saw some of your pottery at the gift shop up at the hotel. You're very talented.'

'Thank you. I live up in the hills above the village. Drop in on me any time you like.'

'I'll do that.'

Jock smiled at her again.

Effie gazed up at him in a dazed way. 'Come now,' she said.

'Can't. I promised the policeman I'd drop in for a dram.'

'I know Hamish. I'll come with you.'

'Not this time. It's man's talk. But I'll see you around.'

Effie retreated, cursing herself. She had been too pushy. But she would act differently the next time. And, oh, there would be a next time. She hardly noticed the walk home. This time she was at her own wedding with Jock at her side. The church bells rang out over Loch-dubh, and the villagers threw rose petals. 'I loved you that first moment I saw you,' Jock murmured.

'Oh, it's yourself,' said Hamish, letting Jock into the kitchen. 'Where's your stuff?'

'In my car.'

'You surely didnae drive the few yards from Mrs Dunne's?'

'No, but it's a good place to put my paints when I'm taking a break.'

'Sit down,' said Hamish. 'I'll get the whisky out.'

Jock looked around the kitchen. It was a narrow room with cupboards and fridge along one wall and a wood-burning stove, which was sending out a blast of heat.

'I'm surprised you've got the fire on today,' said Jock.

'It's got a back boiler. I'm heating up water for a shower.'

'Wouldn't it be easier to have an immersion heater?'

'Thae things cost a mint.' Hamish put a bottle of whisky, a jug of water and two glasses on the table. 'Besides, it'll be a long time afore we see a summer like this again.'

He poured out two measures. 'Water?'

'Just a splash.'

Hamish sat down opposite him.

'Where are your animals?' asked Jock.

'Somewhere around,' said Hamish, who had no intention of telling his visitor that the dog and the cat had eaten well and were now stretched out on his bed. The Currie sisters had started telling him he was behaving like an old maid. Even Archie Macleod had commented the other day that it looked as if Hamish was married to his dog and cat.

'How's the painting going?' asked Hamish.

'It was going fine until I got interrupted by a pushy woman.'

'Mrs Wellington, the minister's wife?'

'No, another artist. Effie Garrard.'

'That quiet wee thing. I'd never have thought of her as being pushy.'

'Oh, maybe I'm being hard on the woman.'

'How pushy?' asked Hamish with his usual insatiable highland curiosity.

304

'Let me see. She asked me to drop in on her any time. Then she wanted me to go back with her there and then. I said I was coming to see you, and she said she would come as well. I told her it was man talk and got rid of her.'

'Maybe she's lonelier than I thought,' said Hamish.

Jock laughed. 'You underrate my charms.'

'I believe you're pretty well known. More whisky?'

'Just a little,' said Jock. 'My agent's coming up from Glasgow.'

'I didn't know artists had agents.'

'Well, we do. She takes her cut and finds me a gallery for an exhibition, and the gallery takes fifty percent. I used to do it myself until she found me and offered her services.'

'How long do you think you'll stay up here?'

'I don't know. The light is fascinating, like nowhere else. I hope the good weather holds so I can make the most of it.'

For the next two days, Effie found she could not concentrate on anything. She sat by the front window, looking down the brae to Lochdubh from early morning until late at night, waiting to see if Jock would call.

On the morning of the third day, she found that all her colourful dreams were beginning to get as thin as gossamer. This time she drove down in her little Ford Escort, not wanting to waste time walking, suddenly anxious to see him.

Jock was sitting at his easel, talking animatedly to Angela Brodie and Freda Campbell, the schoolteacher. Both were married, thought Effie sourly, and should be with their husbands. Freda was not long married, too, and to that local reporter, Matthew Campbell.

She waited patiently in her car for them to go. Then Jock began to pack up his things. Effie watched in dismay as they all headed for Angela's cottage.

She sat nervously biting her thumb.

At last, she got out of her car and went to Angela's cottage. The kitchen door was standing open, and she could hear the sounds of laughter. Squaring her small shoulders, she marched straight into the kitchen. Three startled pairs of eyes turned in her direction.

'Hello, Jock,' said Effie, ignoring the other two.

'Hello. What can I do for you?'

'I've got some paintings and would like your opinion. Can you come up and see them?'

'I'm just about to get back to work,' said Jock, getting to his feet. 'Thanks for the company, ladies.'

Effie followed him, practically running to keep up with his long strides. 'What about this evening?' she panted.

'Oh, all right,' said Jock. 'I'll be up at six. I'm meeting friends for dinner.'

She gave him directions and then asked, 'What friends?'

'Run along, Effie. I'll see you later.'

For the rest of that day, Effie scrubbed and dusted until her cottage was shining. She took a bath in the brown peaty water that always came out of the taps and then dressed in a white wool dress and black velvet jacket. For the first time in her life, she wished she had some make-up. She had never worn any before, claiming it blocked up the pores.

Then she sat by the window. At five minutes past six, she was beginning to despair when she saw his car bumping and lurching over the heathery track that led to her cottage.

She flung open the door and stood beaming a welcome.

Jock ducked his head and followed her in. 'Now, where are these paintings of yours?' he said.

'I thought you might like a glass of whisky first.'

'I'm pressed for time.'

Effie had laid out a selection of her small framed paintings on the table. 'Here they are,' she said.

He picked one up and took it to the window and held it up to the light. 'I'm surprised you can do anything in here,' he said. 'There isn't enough light.'

The painting was of a thrush sitting on a branch of berries. The red of the berries glowed.

'This is exquisite,' said Jock. 'You're very good indeed.'

Effie blushed with pleasure.

Jock appeared to have relaxed. He admired painting after painting and then her pieces of pottery. 'Do you have an agent?' he asked. 'These are much too good just to be shown in Patel's and the gift shop.'

'No, I don't have one.'

'My agent, Betty, will be here soon on holiday. I'll bring her along, if you like.'

'Oh, Jock, that would be marvellous.' She had moved so close to him she was practically leaning against his side.

He felt uneasy. 'I've got to go, but I'll let you know when Betty arrives.'

Jock made for the door. 'Where are you having dinner?' asked Effie.

'The Tommel Castle Hotel. Bye.'

He walked out to his car. He stopped for a moment and breathed in deep lungfuls of air. Then he got in and drove off.

Jock was not meeting anyone for dinner. But he decided to treat himself to dinner at the hotel.

He entered the dining room. A beautiful blonde approached him and said, 'Have you come for dinner?'

'Yes.'

'We've one table left,' said the vision. 'Thank goodness the tourists are back.'

'You're a very glamorous maître d',' commented Jock.

'I'm standing in this evening. My parents run this hotel. I'm Priscilla Halburton-Smythe. Our maître d' is off sick.'

She handed him a large menu and said, 'Your waiter will be along in a minute. Would you like a drink?'

'No thanks. I'll order wine with the meal.'

He watched Priscilla as she walked away. What a figure! And that beautiful bell of golden hair that framed her face! There was a remoteness about her which quickened his senses.

He made his meal last, watching while the other diners gradually finished theirs, hoping all the time for another few words with the beauty.

His back was to the window. At one point, he had an uneasy feeling of being watched. He turned round quickly, but there was no one there.

Priscilla at last came into the dining room and approached him. 'Would you like anything else?'

'I would like you to join me for a coffee.'

Priscilla looked amused. 'I've just been hearing about you. You're Jock Fleming.' She sat in a chair opposite him.

'Are you always here?' asked Jock.

'I work in London. I came up yesterday on holiday. I usually fill in for any of the missing staff when I'm here. It's a duty holiday to see my parents, and I find it can get a bit boring if I have nothing to do.'

'I'd like to take you out one evening,' said Jock. 'Just friends,' he added quickly, suddenly noticing she was wearing an engagement ring. 'Where is your fiancé?'

'In London.'

'So what do you say? What about tomorrow night at that Italian place?'

'All right,' said Priscilla with a laugh. 'What time?'

'Eight o'clock suit you?'

'Fine. Now I'd better go and see how they're getting on clearing up the kitchen.'

Outside, Effie scuttled off from her observation post in the bushes opposite the dining room. Who was that woman? Perhaps she was Jock's agent. She would need to find out.